Jackie French wrote her first collection of short stories, *Rain Stones,* living in a shed with a wallaby called Fred, a black snake called Charlie and a wombat called Smudge. Written on a typewriter found at the dump, the manuscript was regularly attacked by Smudge who left his droppings nightly on the keyboard.

Since then, Jackie has written many books for all age groups including *Mind's Eye, Beyond the Boundaries* and the short-listed *Somewhere Around the Corner.* Jackie French lives in a house in the bush and nowadays, the wombats are outside ...

THE · BOOK OF
UNICORNS

JACKIE FRENCH

Angus&Robertson
An imprint of HarperCollins*Publishers*

To Noel and Fabia and their horses
(and to Geoff, too) with love ~ J.F.

Angus&Robertson
An imprint of HarperCollins*Publishers,* Australia

First published in Australia in 1997
Reprinted in 1997 (twice),
by HarperCollins*Publishers* Pty Limited
ACN 009 913 517
A member of the HarperCollins*Publishers* (Australia) Pty Limited Group
http://www.harpercollins.com.au

HarperCollins*Publishers*
25 Ryde Road, Pymble, Sydney, NSW 2073, Australia
31 View Road, Glenfield, Auckland 10, New Zealand
77-85 Fulham Palace Road, London W6 8JB, United Kingdom
Hazelton Lanes, 55 Avenue Road, Suite 2900, Toronto, Ontario M5R 3L2
and 1995 Markham Road, Scarborough, Ontario M1B 5M8, Canada
10 East 53rd Street, New York NY 10032, USA

National Library of Australia Cataloguing-in-Publication data:

French, Jackie.
The book of unicorns.
ISBN 0 207 19115 8.
I. Title.
A823.3
Printed in Australia by Griffin Press on 79gsm Bulky Paperback

10 9 8 7 6 5 4 3   97 98 99

Contents

Warts

It was a bad summer the Christmas the unicorn was born. The grasshoppers leapt across the hills, the trees drooped hot and limp. The creek was dry and Sam's warts had spread all down his thumbs.

Mum turned the steering wheel too sharply onto the gravel drive that led to Gramma's. The car lurched, then bounced on the stones.

'Watch out!' cried Dad. 'At least I know how to drive on gravel roads.'

'I am watching,' muttered Mum. 'What there is to watch for I don't know. Dry stones and dry hills. They look like skulls all gathered together.'

'Only a week,' said Dad. 'Just one week in the whole year, that's all I ask.'

'I agreed to come, didn't I?' asked Mum. 'So stop complaining.'

'You're the one that's complaining,' argued Dad. 'You're the one who ...'

Sam looked out the window and scratched his warts. It all looked the same as last year. Just drier, and the fences drooped a little more, and the creek was bald white rocks instead of water. Last year Gramma had taken him eeling, just like Dad used to do, said Gramma. Gramma's knee had hurt too much for her to leap across the rocks, but she sat on the bank and told him where to throw the line and how to stop the eels snapping at his fingers …

The car lurched into a pothole. 'You should have let me drive,' said Dad.

'It's impossible to avoid every pothole on this road,' said Mum.

'All right, all right. I'll put the blade on the tractor tomorrow and give it a grade.'

'And half a million other things your mother's got for you to do. Which leaves me in the kitchen and Sam …'

'You leave Sam out of it. Sam likes it here.'

'You'd rather have gone to the beach, wouldn't you, Sam?'

'I …' said Sam. The car bounced round the final corner. 'Hey, there's Gramma!'

Gramma was sitting on the verandah. She looked like she'd been sitting there for a while. She looked up in surprise at the car and its attendant dust.

'Gramma!' yelled Sam.

'Why … Sam,' said Gramma. She looked like she was pleased to have the name right. 'What a lovely surprise.'

'It's not a surprise, Gramma! You knew we were coming!'

'Yes. Of course,' said Gramma. She stepped down the stairs carefully, holding onto the rail. 'It's lovely to see you. Lovely.'

'Mother, I rang last night. Don't you remember?'

'Of course I remember,' said Gramma, holding up her cheek for a kiss. 'You come on in. I'll get some lunch ready.'

'I'll get some lunch ready,' said Gramma for the fourth time, as they wandered round the dusty garden.

Mum sighed and cast Dad a look. 'I'll get it,' she said.

'Oh will you, dear? That'd be nice,' said Gramma absently. She picked a grasshopper off what was left of a rose bush, and wandered over to the apple tree. She fingered the apples.

There were a lot of apples this year, thought Sam, but they'd drop off before they were ripe. They always did.

'Now tell me, Sam,' said Gramma vaguely. 'How is school going?'

Sam sighed. Gramma had asked how school was going twice already. He'd told her 'fine' before. Suddenly he decided to tell the truth.

'Lousy,' said Sam.

Gramma blinked.

'The kids laugh at me because of my warts,' said Sam.

Dad shifted uncomfortably.

'They're all over my hands,' said Sam. 'Elspeth Motrell said she wouldn't share a desk with me last term, in case I touched her with my warts.'

'The doctor burnt them off but they just grow again,' said Dad.

Gramma looked confused. 'Who wouldn't sit next to you?' she asked.

'Elspeth,' said Sam.

'You don't know her, Mother,' said Dad.

'No, that's right,' said Gramma. 'Is she a nice girl? She doesn't sound very nice.' Gramma paused. 'I'll just go and make some lunch.'

'It's okay,' said Sam. 'Mum's getting it.'

'That's nice of her,' said Gramma.

Sam grew bored. He wandered into the kitchen after Mum.

'What's for lunch?' he asked.

Mum slammed the fridge door. 'Slimey lettuce, stale Jatz crackers, a chop that should have been thrown out a week ago. And two thousand eggs.'

'Guess the chooks are laying well,' said Sam.

'What's for lunch?' Dad peered through the screen door.

'Scrambled eggs,' said Mum, grabbing a saucepan with so much force the cupboard shook. 'That's what we're having for dinner, too. That's all there is in the house. Look, isn't it time you faced it? Your mother can't cope out here by herself. You have to do something.'

Dad nodded slowly.

'Don't just nod,' said Mum. 'I'm sick of it! We come down here for what's supposed to be a holiday and you spend all your time trying to catch up on a year's worth of repairs, and half the time at home you're feeling guilty because she's down here alone. It's time we put a stop to it!'

'We'll talk about it after dinner,' said Dad. 'I think Mother realises now she's not coping. Look, do you mind scrambled eggs tonight, too? I'll pop into town tomorrow and stock up.'

'We'll manage,' said Mum.

Sam sneaked off outside.

That was before the unicorn was born.

No one knew the foal was coming, except maybe its mother, the old white mare down by the fence near the creek. Mum and Dad didn't know, and Sam didn't know. He didn't even know Gramma had a horse. She hadn't had one last Christmas or the one before, much less one that was in foal.

Even Gramma couldn't have known. She was too confused to remember things like horses giving birth. But somehow she did know, because she was hobbling down to the fence to this big, old, hungry looking horse just laying there in the dust, and suddenly she was yelling.

'Sam! Sam!'

Sam ran. 'What is it, Gramma? Is it a snake? Have you hurt yourself?'

'Look,' said Gramma. 'Just look.'

Sam looked.

The foal had skinny legs. All foals had skinny legs, but not like this. These legs were thin like chopsticks. Even without knowing much about horses Sam could see they weren't made right. The head was too small too with this funny bony thing pointing out of its forehead, and the eyes looked blank and blue, not like proper horse eyes at all. Even the body looked lopsided.

'It's a unicorn,' said Gramma proudly, batting a grasshopper out of her eye.

'There's no such thing as unicorns, Gramma,' said Sam. She'd be telling him about the tooth fairy next. Sometimes Sam thought that Gramma still believed that he was three years old.

The foal tried to stand. Its legs were still too weak. It stumbled and gave a bleating cry, then just lay there, panting.

The mare sniffed it. She whinnied, a funny crazy sound. She struggled to her feet, then walked slowly down the fence line.

'Where's she going?' cried Sam. 'Why's she leaving her baby?'

Gramma blinked. 'I don't know,' she said slowly. 'Maybe ... well, I don't know.'

'Is it 'cause it's different?' whispered Sam. He reached out and stroked the creature's head. It felt damp, but very warm.

'Maybe,' said Gramma. She sat beside Sam and pulled the whimpering foal onto her lap. It came easily, like it had no bones. Its head drooped onto Gramma's dress as she stroked its too-long neck.

'What do we do now, Gramma?' asked Sam.

Gramma seemed to look into the distance for a while. She didn't speak. She just stroked and stroked till finally Sam couldn't wait any more.

'Gramma?' he asked again. 'What are we going to do?'

Gramma blinked, like she'd been a long way off. She looked at Sam like she was surprised to see him there. 'Sam ...' said Gramma. She looked down at the ugly foal. 'Well, I reckon we'll take him back to the house,' she said slowly. 'Put him in a box by the stove like the poddy lambs. We used to have lots of poddy lambs ...'

'But what'll he eat?' demanded Sam.

Something seemed to seep back into Gramma, something strong and sure. 'Why, I reckon I'll have to milk the old girl if she won't feed her foal,' said Gramma. 'I used to milk cows often enough.'

'But this is a horse, Gramma!'

'I reckon I can milk a horse,' said Gramma, even more firmly now.

'And feed the baby with a bottle?'

'And feed him with a bottle,' agreed Gramma. 'Here, help me to my feet. It's my knees. They don't work like they used to. Nothing works much like it did before.'

Gramma settled the limp foal into a big cardboard fruit box by the stove. It could hold its head up now, but still didn't look like it could ever stand. Its blue blank eyes stared unblinking at the world.

'It's a freak. It's deformed,' said Mum flatly. 'It should be put down.' She turned to Dad. 'Don't you think so ...'

'I agree,' said Dad. 'Look Mother, I'll take it out the back and ...'

'It stays here,' said Gramma firmly.

'But ...'

'I said no,' said Gramma. Dad looked rattled and Mum just stared. 'And while we're at it,' said Gramma. 'There'll be no more talk about me going to a nursing home. Not while I've still got my strength. Now, what's for dinner?'

'Scrambled eggs,' said Mum. 'Just like for lunch. That's all there was in the fridge. Just eggs and stuff that should have been thrown out. We'll go into town tomorrow and buy some ...'

Gramma snorted. 'Scrambled eggs is no fit food for a growing boy. Is that what you feed Sam at home? Sam, you get my axe. It's down the back of the shed. We're having roast chook for tea.'

Gramma stuffed the chook with stale bread, and a chopped onion from the back of the cupboard and herbs from the dusty garden out the back. Then she hobbled down to the fence by the creek with a bucket. Sam carried her stool.

Gramma lowered herself down onto the stool slowly. She stretched out her legs. 'Used to be my knees only ached when it rained,' she said. 'Then they ached in winter too. Now they ache all the time. And most of the rest of me.'

'What's wrong with them, Gramma?' asked Sam.

'Arthritis, the doctor says,' said Gramma. 'But I reckon it's just I'm getting old.' She reached for the mare's udder. The mare just stood there, gazing out at the bare paddock, indifferent.

The first squirt of milk battered at the edges of the bucket and ran down the side. It pooled in a small blue puddle at the bottom. 'Firm but gentle, see?' said Gramma, as she alternated strokes from teat to teat.

Sam nodded. 'Can I have a go?'

'Maybe tomorrow,' said Gramma. 'Or the next day,

when she's used to being milked. You remind me to get some hay in town tomorrow, and a bag of stud mix too. We need to feed her up.'

Sam watched, fascinated. 'Does it feel different from a cow?' he asked.

'Cow or horse, it's all the same,' said Gramma, watching the thin blue milk squirt into the bucket. 'I suppose you could milk an elephant too if you had to. I knew a bloke once who milked an echidna.'

'Yuk. What did he do with the milk?'

'Sent it to the uni. Someone was going to analyse it, see what the echidna had been eating. But he drank a bit first, just to see what it tasted like.'

'What did it taste like?'

'Ants,' said Gramma. 'There we are. I reckon that's enough for now. Can you carry the bucket as well as the stool, Sam? My hands are shaky. I'd hate to spill it now.'

It took the foal a few minutes to work out how to suck from a bottle. It drank slowly, as though it hurt to swallow. It shivered, even though the kitchen was warm.

'Hot-water bottle,' said Gramma. 'It's in the drawer under the sink. Yes, that's the one. Thanks, Sam. Now if you'd just fill the kettle we'll boil it up …'

Gramma wrapped the hot-water bottle in an old towel and tucked it next to the unicorn, and covered them both with a blanket. The foal rested its head against the side of the box and closed its pale blank eyes.

'Gramma?'

'Yes, Sam.'

'Is it going to live?'

'It'll live,' said Gramma.

Dad insisted on driving into town next day, even though Gramma said she was quite capable.

'I've been driving into town for fifty years. It's still the same way in it's always been. It hasn't changed,' Gramma complained from the front seat beside Dad.

Dad veered around another pothole. 'The way into town hasn't changed, but I think you have, Mother,' he said warily. 'The back tyre was flat this morning. And the battery was flat too. I bet you haven't driven the car for months.'

'It's been a while since I drove,' admitted Gramma. 'I haven't been feeling the best. But I'm better now.'

'How have you been getting groceries?' asked Sam.

'The postman brings them down,' said Gramma. 'You know, Len McIntyre, your father was at school with his brother. He brings my groceries out. When I remember to let him know what to bring.'

'Look Mother …' said Dad.

'No,' said Gramma. 'I'm not going into a nursing

home. I'm not coming down to the city to live with you either. But thank you anyway. Now stop here … no, to the right. You pop in to the baker's and get the bread while I pick up some stud mix for the mare.'

The foal was sleeping when they got home, but it lifted its head when they came in.

'See, it's getting stronger,' said Gramma.

'I still think …' said Dad, and then he stopped. He sighed and began to put away the groceries instead.

'Where's Mum?' asked Sam.

'Off in a snit somewhere,' said Dad. 'All I ask is a few days down here once a year, but …'

'Hey, Gramma! The grasshoppers have gone!'

Dad peered out the window. 'My word, they have too. I reckon they've decided they've eaten everything they could round here and just moved on.'

''Bout time, too,' said Gramma.

Sam and Gramma took a bucket of stud mix down to the mare after lunch. Sam carried the bucket. Gramma seemed to walk straighter today. 'Arthritis always gets better in dry weather,' she said. 'I reckon this is about as dry as it comes.'

The mare thrust her nose into the stud mix and ate gratefully.

'I'm sorry old thing,' said Gramma. 'I should have

been feeding you long before this. You get stuck into it.'

'Where did she come from, Gramma?' asked Sam.

'Sale up at town,' said Gramma. 'No one wanted her. She was going to be bought for dog meat when I bought her. Didn't cost me much. Didn't know she was in foal till later.'

'Poor old thing,' said Sam, stroking her nose. 'I wish she'd liked her baby though.'

Darkness seemed to sit on the house, squeezing out all sound. It was too quiet, thought Sam, lying in the narrow bed that used to be Dad's, watching the trees droop against the stars. You kept thinking that a car would go by or a dog would bark or someone yell. But no one did.

Something squeaked, so suddenly the silence almost cracked. Sam sat up. What was it?

The sound came again.

Sam pulled the sheet up around his chest. Should he get up and investigate? But it was probably just a mouse, or Gramma going down to the bathroom or …

… or a rat — a great big rat. Rats attacked baby animals didn't they? Maybe it would hurt the foal.

Maybe it was the foal crying in its sleep …

The noise stopped. Sam waited for it to start again. But it didn't. A possum screamed out in the trees, then there was silence.

Sam dozed. Suddenly his eyes opened again. A different noise …

Sam slid out of bed and felt for his slippers. The moonlight washed gently through the room. He was glad there was no need to turn on the light. The light might wake up Mum and Dad.

The passageway was quiet too. His slippers flopped gently on the old linoleum.

Mum sat by the foal's box. Its head rested tiredly in her lap. She looked up as he came in. For a horrible moment Sam thought the foal was dead, then he realised its eyes were open, pale as old glass in the moonlight. Mum stroked its head.

'It was whimpering,' she explained.

'I know. I heard it.' Sam squatted down beside them. 'I thought you didn't like the foal,' said Sam.

'I didn't like it,' said Mum. 'But it looks different tonight. Sort of sweet.'

It looked the same to Sam. Floppy and weak and that strange almost glowing white. Its head lolled back onto the edge of the box. Mum shifted a bit of blanket under it like a pillow.

'Have you been here long?' asked Sam.

'A while,' said Mum. 'It's been peaceful, just sitting here. You forget what silence is like at home.'

The possum shrieked again, nearer this time.

Something ran across the roof. Mum smiled. 'Not that it's really silent,' she said. 'There're all sorts of noises if you listen to them. I heard an owl a little while ago. Maybe it's hunting the possum. And there was a funny bird call, like something running down the scales but not quite getting there. I don't know what it was.'

'Dad'd know,' said Sam.

'I'll ask him later,' said Mum

They sat quietly for a while. The foal managed to lift its head. It whinnied again, softly, but this time it didn't sound in pain. 'Is there any more milk?' whispered Mum. 'I'll heat up a bottle for it.'

'Gramma left some in the fridge,' said Sam.

Mum put the kettle on, then tiptoed to the fridge. 'You pop back to bed,' she said to Sam. 'You're getting cold.'

'You don't need a hand?' asked Sam.

'No,' said Mum. 'I'm fine.'

Gramma made baked bean jaffles for breakfast. The foal lifted its head and watched for a moment before sinking back into its box. Mum ate her jaffle slowly. Sam knew she didn't like baked beans.

'Elva?' she said to Gramma.

'Yes?'

'Is there someone around who does odd jobs?

Someone who could grade the road for you, fix the fences, stuff like that?'

Gramma paused with the dish mop in her hand. 'Willie McRae,' she said. 'He's always after a job of work.'

'Do you think he'd come down today? Gary and I would pay him of course,' said Mum quickly. 'I know it's hard to afford help on your pension. But if he could grade the road ...'

'I was going to grade the road,' said Dad. 'I'll stick the blade on the tractor this morning. I'd have done it yesterday but we had to go into town ...'

'I know. But I was thinking ...'

'What?'

'Maybe we could go for a walk instead. Up to the old hut by the waterfall.'

'The waterfall'll be dry,' warned Gramma.

'I know. But it'd be interesting anyway. I've never been there. You've told me about that hut so many times, how you used to go up there and camp when you were a kid. I'd like to see it.'

Dad hesitated.

'I'll ring Willie after breakfast,' said Gramma. 'You pack up some lunch. It's a long walk up to the hut.'

Dad grinned. 'The old hut,' he said. 'I haven't thought about it for years. You coming, Sam?'

'Sam and I are going to strain the fence down by the creek,' said Gramma. 'And we have to feed the mare and give the foal its bottles. Off you go. We'll expect you when we see you.'

It had been a good holiday, thought Sam, as the car drove down the newly graded track. He turned back for a final look. Gramma was still waving, the ugly foal in her lap. It could hold its head up now, though it still couldn't stand.

'And so it's all sorted out with Willie,' Mum was saying in the front. 'He'll finish re-straining the fences this week, then after that he'll come every Thursday.'

Dad nodded.

'And you'll send him a cheque once a month. I mean it's not like we can't afford it,' said Mum.

Dad nodded again. 'And he's getting Matt Godwin at the hardware store to get someone to paint the house. It'll be good to see the old place looking good again.' He glanced back at the house. 'It's a long time to Christmas,' he said to himself.

'There's always Easter,' said Mum offhandedly. 'Why don't we come down then? I mean it's a long drive, but we've both got some leave up our sleeves ...'

'But we always go to the beach at Easter,' said Dad. 'You said it's not fair to Sam to come back here so soon.'

He looked back at Sam. 'Do you mind coming down here again, instead of the beach?' he asked.

'I don't mind,' said Sam. 'Besides, I want to see the foal.'

'How's the foal?' asked Sam. It was the same question he always asked, every Sunday night when Dad rang Gramma.

'It's fine,' said Gramma. 'It almost stood up by itself yesterday. I'm getting Willie to rig something up for it. You'll see when you come down. How's school?'

'Okay,' said Sam. 'I'm in the basketball team. Hey! Guess what, Gramma?'

'What?'

'My warts are gone. Just like that. I woke up yesterday and they were gone.'

'Gone where?'

'I dunno. They must've dropped off. I looked in the bed but I couldn't see them.'

'They must've flown away,' said Gramma. 'Warts do that sometimes.'

'How's the old mare?' asked Sam.

'She's getting fat,' said Gramma. 'All this grass. It's green as a new carpet after all this rain. You wouldn't think she was the same horse. Look, I have to go. I've got a cake in the oven, I promised to take it to the tennis club tomorrow. You take care won't you? Love you, Sam.'

'Love you, Gramma,' said Sam. 'Give my love to the foal.'

'I will,' said Gramma.

Gramma's house looked different as they drove down the drive that Easter. Someone had painted it pale blue and there was grass now instead of dust. The hills looked like green balls waiting for someone to play.

Gramma was in the vegie garden. She waved as they came over. 'Just picking corn for lunch,' she said. 'It's a good garden this year, isn't it? I had Willie put it in just after you left.'

'I've never seen corn that big!' said Sam. 'Those cobs are as long as a cricket bat, almost.'

'Unicorn dung,' grinned Gramma. 'I bring a bagful down every morning.'

'Gramma, there's no such things as unicorns.'

'Sure there are. Unicorn dung's the best fertiliser there is. Come on up to the house and I'll show you the foal. You won't believe how he's grown.'

The ugly foal had grown, thought Sam, but not much. It looked like it'd never be a full-sized horse. It was like it didn't have the energy to grow. As though it was saving all its energy — for what? Sam thought. The foal gazed slightly to one side of them with its milky eyes.

'Looking good, isn't he?' demanded Gramma.

'Yes,' said Sam doubtfully. 'Is that what you had rigged up, Gramma?' He pointed to the cage structure around the foal.

'That's it,' said Gramma proudly. 'You see the sling goes round its body and holds it up so its feet can touch the ground without any weight on them. Then the cage supports the sling. When the foal tries to walk the wheels go round and the foal can move along ... well, it moves a bit anyway. That way it can graze for a couple of hours all by itself. I keep moving the sling so it doesn't get too sore. How's school?'

'It's great,' said Sam. And it was, sort of.

Gramma grinned. 'Let's see your hands.'

Sam held them out. 'No warts,' he said. 'Not a single one.'

'I bet they don't come back either,' said Gramma. 'You're immune to warts now. There's something else I want to show you too.'

'What, Gramma?'

'You wait and see,' said Gramma. She led the way to the shed. It looked better now, thought Sam, with the broken palings replaced and new posts put in on one side. Gramma pulled one of the doors aside. 'Look,' she said.

Sam looked. 'Gramma! It's a farm bike!'

'Good as new,' said Gramma. 'Except it isn't. I got it from Bob Braddon up in town, who got it from … well, never mind that. Point is it still goes. Willie uses it when he's out fencing, but I thought you'd like to have a go while you're here.'

'Gramma!'

'Now you ask your parents first. And make sure you wear a helmet and long sleeves and jeans and boots … and no haring off at a hundred miles an hour either. You be careful.'

'I'll be careful,' promised Sam, staring at the machine. 'Wow!'

Gramma laughed.

Paddocks were made for farm bikes, thought Sam, feeling the tussocks bump beneath him. You felt like you could ride forever — over the ford in the creek the water spraying in your face, down the track to the fence and up the fence line. You could see the highway from here through the thin barrier of trees along the fence, cars and trucks and the odd motorbike beetling off to who knows where.

Sam paused, as a semi slowed, then drew off the road a little way ahead. Sam accelerated to catch up with it.

'Is anything wrong?' he called out through the open

window. 'I could ride back to the house if you like and ring the garage.'

The truckie leant out of the window and grinned. 'No worries, kid. I'm just stopping for a snack. Most of us stop along here now.' He gestured out the window.

Sam looked around. The truckie must be right. There was a clear track now beside the gum trees, long enough for a semi to park and be quite off the road.

'Why here?' asked Sam. 'I mean no one used to stop here.'

The truckie shrugged and looked embarrassed. 'Dunno,' he said. 'Started last Christmas, I reckon. This bloke broke down here, or so he thought. But when he tried to start her up again she ran like a dream. Since then people just stop here.'

'Why not down the road though,' said Sam. 'I mean there's a proper rest stop there with a toilet and everything.'

The truckie looked even more embarrassed. 'This spot's different,' he said. 'Most of the blokes'll tell you that. You stop for ten minutes here and shut your eyes and it'll seem like you've slept the whole night through. You don't get accidents if you stop for a bit of a break here. Least that's what they say.' He passed a thermos out to Sam. 'You like a drink, kid?'

'No thanks.' Sam shook his head. 'I need to get back for lunch.'

'You live round here?' asked the truckie.

'No. Just staying with my gramma.'

'You're lucky,' said the truckie. He paused. 'I've got a kid your age. It makes my heart break sometimes thinking of him cramped in the city in the holidays.' The truckie grinned. 'Not that he seems to mind. The only thing that bothers him are these great plantar warts on his foot. Says it stops him playing soccer.'

The bike began to mutter. Sam gave it more accelerator. 'You should bring him out with you some time,' said Sam. He hesitated. 'I'd better get back,' he said. 'Gramma'll be expecting me. We have to feed the ...' He stopped.

'See you,' said the truckie. 'It's got a good feel to it, this place. Feels like ... well, I dunno what it feels like. But it does you good. You must love it down here.'

'It's a good place,' said Sam.

'I reckon,' said the truckie.

Gramma was picking apples when Sam rode up. He parked the bike in the shed and fetched another box to help her.

'Thanks, Sam,' said Gramma, piling another armful of

apples into the new box. 'That's six boxes full so far. I'll be making apple jelly till the cows come home with this lot. You'd better take some back with you.'

Sam nodded, though he didn't like apple jelly much. 'I thought the apples all fell off this tree before they ripened.'

'Always have before,' said Gramma. 'I've been feeding it this year though. Couple of buckets of unicorn manure every week. I reckon that's all it needed, just a bit of feeding.' She looked at her watch. 'Time for lunch,' she said. 'I have to go into town later. It's my line dancing afternoon.'

'Your what?' asked Sam.

'Texas line dancing. It's the latest thing. We all get into these two lines and do the same steps. It's twice a week now at the Returned Services Club. Don't you have Texas line dancing up in the city?'

'I don't know,' said Sam. 'It sounds sort of ... energetic. Can you manage it okay, Gramma?'

'Of course I can,' said Gramma. 'I was a bit stiff at first, that's all. But it's done me the world of good. I just needed some more exercise, that's all. How about you come with me? Lots of kids round here do line dancing.'

'No thanks, Gramma,' said Sam politely. 'I'll just stay here. Maybe I'll take the foal for a walk.'

Gramma looked at him sharply. 'It doesn't walk much,' she reminded him.

'Well, a sort of a push then. Maybe down to the creek — the grass looks all soft there. Maybe it'll like it.'

'It probably will,' said Gramma. 'Probably tastes different from the grass up here. Things like that must mean something to a horse.'

'Is the old mare still down there, Gramma?' Sam wondered what the horse thought of her foal now.

Gramma shook her head. 'I gave her away,' she said. 'You don't mind do you? Funny thing, these people were just driving past and this girl saw her and fell in love with her.'

Sam snorted. 'Girls always fall in love with horses,' he said. 'She probably thinks she's going to win a ribbon at the Easter show with the poor old thing.'

'Not this kid,' said Gramma. 'She didn't even want to ride her. I told her the mare was too old to do much with, but it didn't matter to her. She had some sort of palsy I reckon. Her hands were shaking like mad. I think she just wanted a pet — her parents asked if they could buy her. I said she hadn't cost me much, they could have her if they promised to take good care of her. I think they will. They looked that type.'

'I hope they had a decent paddock to put her in,' said Sam.

'They said there was a paddock just down the road from their place,' said Gramma. 'Hired a horse float for

her and everything. You know, it's funny, but I could
have sworn she was in foal again. Impossible. I mean at
her age, and there hasn't been another horse around
for donkey's years. I warned them she might be, but
they didn't seem to mind. I hope there wasn't
anything too bad wrong with the kid. Maybe she's
better now.'

'Maybe she is,' said Sam.

It was peaceful in the house with everyone gone,
Gramma off to her whatsit dancing up in town, and
Dad had hauled Mum off to meet some old friends of
his. They had a property the other side of town, but no
kids his age, so it sounded pretty boring to Sam.

The foal was lying under the old apple tree. It didn't
even try to struggle as Sam approached, just looked at
him sort of sideways with its milky eyes. Sam wondered
how much it could see. Maybe it just saw differently,
that was all.

He stroked its head. The hair felt smooth, not like a
horse's at all, sort of moist and flat. Like a seal's fur,
thought Sam, who'd never felt a seal.

'Come on, boy,' he said. 'Let's go for a walk.'

The foal leant against his arm as he fixed his harness,
limp and impassive. Like it was waiting, thought Sam,
but waiting for what? Its feet pulled tentatively at the

harness, far too slow and delicate to move it much, so Sam had to push it all the way.

The creek was thick with autumn shadows and the faint smell of cooling rocks and water. Sam unstrapped the foal, and made sure he was settled comfortably on the grass. The foal sniffed and whinnied once, a short sharp cry like a small baby's, then tore a mouthful of grass. It chewed it slowly then seemed to go to sleep.

Sam lay down as well. The grass was soft and thin on the sandy ground. He could see the casuarina needles toss against the sky, still faintly red tinged from autumn pollen. He thought he heard the foal whimper again. He listened for a moment more, but it was silent.

Sam closed his eyes.

It was a funny dream. He was by the creek, but the casuarinas were dark green now. The creek looked sort of different too, as though the rocks had shifted in a flood … or two … or three … but things always looked different in a dream.

He wasn't alone. There were other people too. Two men, a woman. They were important people. Somehow in the background of his dream he knew they were important. They had problems to discuss. Important problems. They couldn't agree. So he'd said, 'Lets take the whole day off. I'll take you down and show you Gramma's unicorn.'

They'd laughed. 'There's no such thing as unicorns,' one of the men had said. But still they'd come down to Gramma's, down to the creek, down to see the unicorn …

The men had taken their jackets off. The woman's shoes lay by the bank. Now they sat on the soft grass … but it was thicker now, thought Sam, and there were tiny orchid heads among the green and the problems seemed to dissolve into the flash of water …

The unicorn whinnied softly and Sam woke up.

Sam walked slowly back up the track to the house, pulling the unicorn behind him.

A Present
for
Aunt Addie

ou're old enough,' said Dad thoughtfully.

Harry looked up from the TV. 'Old enough for what?' he demanded warily.

Dad was silent for a moment. Harry expected him to say to clean out the chook shed. To bring the steers down from the back paddock by yourself. To make sure your room is tidy without telling you all the time. But he didn't. He looked out the window instead.

'To visit Aunt Addie,' said Dad at last. 'There's something that she needs.'

Harry looked out the window, too. There was nothing to see. Or nothing special anyway. Just the hills beyond the lucerne paddock, hazy in the blue green heat.

'Who's Aunt Addie?' he asked. 'Hey, she must be your sister if she's my aunt. I didn't know you had a sister.'

'I don't,' said Dad.

'Mum's sister then,' said Harry. 'But I thought her only sisters were Aunt Sue and Auntie Sheila.'

'Not your mother's sister,' said Dad.

'Well, what then?' asked Harry exasperated. This wasn't like Dad at all. 'You mean she's not really an aunt. Just a friend I'm supposed to call Auntie but she isn't really related to us.'

'She's related to us,' said Dad. 'Oh my word, she's related to us.'

'Well, what then?' demanded Harry.

Dad reached over and turned off the TV. The chooks out the back clucked in the sudden silence.

'She's my great-great-aunt,' said Dad slowly. 'Your great-great-great-aunt that'd make her. I think that's right. I get confused with all these greats.'

'But that'd make her ...' Harry stared. 'She can't be that old.'

'Well, she is,' said Dad softly. 'Aunt Addie's very old.'

'Where is she then? In town? In the nursing home? Or the hospital? Heck, she should be in the papers if she's as old as that.'

'No. She's not in the nursing home. Or in the hospital for that matter either. She lives here. On the farm.'

'But I've never seen her.'

'No,' said Dad. 'You haven't seen her yet. She lives up in a hut up past the hills.'

'By herself! Dad she can't! Not an old woman like that! She shouldn't be living by herself.'

'She wants to live by herself,' said Dad.

'But ...' Harry stood up. 'It isn't right. We should visit her at least. See if she's all right. Take her food and stuff.'

'She doesn't need food,' said Dad. 'Aunt Addie grows all she needs. Or gets it somehow, anyway. All she needs is ... well, you'll find out.'

'But ... but someone should at least keep her

company! What if she breaks her leg? Old people's bones are fragile. We learnt that at school …'

Dad held up a hand. 'All right. All right. I said it's time you visited her.'

Harry nodded. 'Well, sure.' He blinked. 'How long is it since you've seen her?'

'Fifteen years,' said Dad. 'It's been fifteen years since I last saw Aunt Addie.'

'What? You haven't seen her since before I was born? Why not?'

'That's the way it turned out,' said Dad.

The hills glared gold in the morning light, as though the sun shone from them as well. Not much feed, thought Harry automatically. It had all dried up since last month's rain. The sheep lay like sleeping boulders under the scattered stringybarks.

Harry pulled his hat down lower. He wondered if he should have brought some water. It was too dangerous to drink from any of the streams nowadays, what with hydatids and giardia and sheep droppings, but Dad said there was no need to take anything.

It seemed wrong not to take anything though. You always took something when you went to visit people — a cake or jam or a leg of lamb. He'd thought of taking flowers, but they'd have wilted by the time he got there, and if anyone saw him he'd look a burk carrying flowers across a paddock.

Surely there was something Aunt Addie needed. Maybe she was really independent, like Saul's grandma. Saul's grandma just lived on sardines and bread and powdered milk and what she grew in the garden. She didn't even need lights because she went to bed when it got dark. Saul's mum wanted her to go down to the nursing home in town, but Saul's gran wouldn't budge. But even she needed to buy the sardines and milk and flour …

Maybe it was just company Aunt Addie needed. Or some repairs maybe? Or digging in the garden? But how would Dad know if he hadn't seen her for fifteen years?

Harry shooed the flies from the back of his neck. They were probably thirsty, too, but let them find their own water and leave his sweat alone.

Why hadn't Dad let him take his motorbike? It was a Honda 110, he'd only got it last Christmas, only two thousand and twenty k's when he got it from Phil up in town, though he'd put a lot more on it since then. Phil was moving down the coast and couldn't use a motorbike down there. But Dad had said he'd never find Aunt Addie on a motorbike, which was crazy, 'cause a bike could carry you anywhere, just about.

Walking was crazy in this heat. Dad was crazy. The whole thing was crazy, too.

How could he have an aunt living at the back of the property that no one ever saw? He'd explored the whole place hundreds of time, and he'd never even seen a hint of someone living there.

It was impossible. A woman that old. It had to be a joke. But Dad wasn't one for joking much.

Aunt Addie needed something Dad had said. But what?

Harry looked around him. Which way had Dad said? Back of the hill paddock, up the gully between the second and third hills. Then just keep going till you find it. It'd be even hotter up there, no breeze at all. Who'd want to live up there?

Had he ever come this way before? He couldn't remember. Surely he must have. He'd come up into the hills lots of times. He must have come this way before …

The sheep looked at him curiously, then looked away, bored by the heat. Humans were only interesting if they carried hay or were followed by dogs.

Gold grass gave way to rocks, leaning out of the hill like they'd fallen backwards and hadn't managed to rise again. The gully rose in wide sharp lips of stone, ascending in what would be cascades of water when it rained. The rock was dry now, grey instead of brown. A frog creaked hopefully behind a boulder, then was still. There must be damp spots somewhere, thought Harry, looking at the green fringes round the rocks. The musky scent of black snake floated up from the hot rocks. If that frog didn't watch out it'd be a snake's dinner, thought Harry.

Up, up, up the rocks. Surely no one could live up here. Dad must be mad.

Maybe that was it. Maybe Dad was going bonkers. You heard of people going bonkers with stress and worry when it wouldn't rain and the cattle prices were down. Except that cattle prices weren't bad at the moment, thought Harry, and there was still enough feed. Dad was a good farmer. Even in the bad drought the paddocks weren't overstocked. There'd still been hay in the shed at the end of the drought, thought Harry proudly. And their pasture was coming back, now that it had finally rained, almost as good as it had been four years before.

More rocks. The gully closed around him. Crikey, you couldn't even build a hut up here it was so steep, much less live here. What would you do for water? You'd break your ankle every time you went outside.

Suddenly the gully forked. Harry hesitated, wondering which way to go. It was all right for Dad to say, 'Just keep going till you get there.' What if he'd forgotten the way? It had been fifteen years since he'd been to Aunt Addie's, after all.

Straight up or to the left … well, not straight up. No

one lived on the top of the hill, you'd see the house miles away. It must be to the left.

Harry turned and began to clamber up again.

It was more level going now, as though this gully ran between the first hill and a higher one above. It was almost flat, but even hotter. Incredibly hot ...

The air swam round him. The rock seemed to swim as well. Heat, heat, heat ... The hills rose steeply on either side, almost too steep for grass now. It was thinner, longer, almost like hair, ungrazed by sheep or wallaby.

Round a corner, round another — the gully seemed to flatten even further. For the first time water seeped between the rocks, pooling at the lips. The smell of moisture almost overcame the scent of rock.

Another corner and another. Sweat stung his eyes and the world blurred even more. Surely it wouldn't hurt to have a drink up here, so far from the sheep and roos. He'd bet even the wombats didn't come up here. No animals at all ... He'd only drink a little where it seeped out cool from the crevices, not from the pools. Surely the water wouldn't be too bad straight from underground.

Harry knelt and touched his fingers to the water. It was colder than he'd expected, like frozen aluminium on your skin. Now if he could catch some water as it seeped down from the rock.

Something flickered in the pool. It was white and large. A cloud, thought Harry dreamily. A cloud reflected in the pool. Then the white thing moved and he saw it wasn't a cloud at all.

It was an animal. A large animal.

Harry stood up slowly.

The animal looked at him. It was a little shorter than he was, so the green eyes looked almost into his. It was white, pure white, not like a cloud at all. Clouds always had shades of grey and blue. Its tail hung almost to the ground. Its teeth were yellow, stained with grass. Its horn was whiter than its body, twisted round into a straight sharp point.

The unicorn whinnied and bent its head to drink.

Harry wiped his wet hands across his face. He had sunstroke, that's what it was. He was hallucinating, dreaming in the heat.

Maybe he wasn't dreaming. Dreams weren't as real as this. Maybe someone was making a movie. That was it. A movie with a unicorn. You could do all sorts of things with make-up and special effects and computers nowadays. They were making a unicorn movie in the gully and that's why Dad had sent him here …

It still didn't make sense.

The unicorn lifted its wet muzzle from the water and

looked at Harry. Its gaze was straight and clear. It tossed its mane, as though to say, 'come on', and trotted up the gully. Its hooves clicked sharply on the rock.

Harry followed.

Around another bend, and then another. The air was fresher somehow. The gully smelt ... strange. Not just the scents of horse and water, but something more, like that stuff Mum squirted in the bathroom sometimes, but different from that, too.

Suddenly the unicorn stopped. Harry stopped as well. The world was shimmering as though it wasn't real. But it was real. It was.

The gully had opened slightly, so creek flats spread on each side. They were green, impossibly green, the grass like a green blanket spread between the hills. Cliffs rose steeply on three sides, too steep for grass, tufted with ferns about the crevices. A miniature waterfall tumbled from a dark hole halfway up the cliff, dropping to a small dark pool below. The spray drifted through the clearing like tiny specks of sun so the clearing seemed to shiver as they danced.

A hut sat at the far end of the clearing. It was old, like sketches he'd seen in a book at school. The roof was made from wood as well, square slabs like bits of greyish toast, overlapped together. The hut itself was small and square and made from long fat slabs of wood, like they'd been cut from the tree and nailed together willy-nilly. Some sort of vine clambered over every wall, dotted with flowers, like roses, but too fat to be roses, thought Harry. Surely roses didn't droop and glow like that.

There was no verandah, no windows, no TV aerial or power lines. Just wooden shutters over what must be gaps in the wall, a chimney that smoked small puffs of white, and — the garden.

Why hadn't he seen the smoke from down below? thought Harry. It didn't make sense. But nothing here made sense.

Especially not the garden.

Half the clearing was a garden, but a funny garden, not like any that he'd ever seen. It shivered in the sunlight, as though the colours melted with the waterspray.

There were no garden beds, no patches of dark soil, no lawn unless you counted the brilliant green around. Just flowers ... and flowers ... and more flowers — bursting from the ground in spires of red and blue and yellow, carpets of blues and golds and pinks stretching at their feet. Their colours seemed to float up to the waterspray and merge into the sunlight, so it was hard to see what was garden or sun. A path ran crazily round and through and in between.

A woman stood in the middle of the garden, a basket of peaches tucked under one arm. Her dress was long, almost to her ankles, a sort of straw colour flecked with pink and white. Her hair was brown and curled round her shoulders. Her skin was very clear and white. Her eyes were the same colour as the unicorn's.

She took a step towards him. 'Ron,' she said. She smiled, took a peach out of her basket and before Harry could react she'd thrown it to him. He caught it automatically.

'It's the first of the season,' said the woman. The unicorn whinnied softly. The woman smiled again. 'One for you as well,' she said. She tossed another peach to the unicorn. It caught it with its yellow teeth and crunched it carefully, spitting the stone out at its feet. The woman looked at Harry again. 'Ron?' she said uncertainly.

Harry shook his head, 'My name's Harry,' he said. 'My father's name is Ron.'

'Then you're Ron's son!' The woman clapped her hands delightedly. 'I'm so very pleased! It's years since Ron was here! So many years … I lose track of time, I think. And here you are, Ron's son!'

'Aunt Addie?' said Harry uncertainly.

'Yes. I am your Aunt Addie.' The woman's smile was clear as the blue flowers.

'But you can't be Aunt Addie! Aunt Addie's old! Dad said ...'

Aunt Addie seemed amused. 'I am Aunt Addie. Come!'

Harry stepped into the shimmering garden.

It was the softness that struck him first. The ground felt soft. The air felt soft, as though it stroked his cheek. Even the sounds seemed softer, muted by the hum of bees, the ripple of the water, as though the flowers whispered in the breeze.

The unicorn stepped after him. Harry glanced up at Aunt Addie, expecting her to shoo it from the garden, before it ate the flowers or trod on something. But the woman simply held out her hand. The unicorn stepped neatly between the flowers and nuzzled at her fingers, then trotted to a bank of green. It began to graze.

Aunt Addie gestured to a seat. It was made of twisted wood, old but not rotted looking either. 'Sit you down, sit down,' she insisted. 'I'll bring you a drink. It's of my own making, and very good this year. You'll see.' Her skirts whispered against the flowers as she went into the hut.

Harry craned his head to look inside. A glimpse of a table spread with cloth much the same colour as Aunt Addie's dress, a bed of pink and white as well, a wooden floor with coloured mats. The door swung shut, then opened as Aunt Addie came out.

She carried an enamelled jug and a thick brown stumpy glass. She handed the glass to Harry, then poured the liquid from the jug. She looked at him expectantly. 'Try it,' she said.

He supposed it was all right to drink. Surely Dad would have told him if Aunt Addie was dangerous. It smelt all right.

Harry sipped.

The liquid tasted like flowers, warm and just a little oversweet. A bird sang deep among the trees. A strange bird. He'd never heard a song like that before. Harry blinked. The trees. Why hadn't he noticed them before? Spreading trees in different shades of green, with broad soft leaves that seemed to welcome sunlight, suck it down.

Harry sipped the drink again. 'It's good,' he said. 'What is it?'

Aunt Addie looked pleased. 'Violet cordial,' she said. 'I just yesterday uncorked it. Will you have some more?'

Harry shook his head. He felt like he'd swallowed sunlight — and like it might be alcoholic, too. 'Maybe just some water,' he said.

Aunt Addie nodded at the pool under the waterfall. 'It's coolest there,' she said.

Harry went slowly over to the waterfall and dipped his cup. The water was colder than the cordial. Harry dipped his cup again, then stared back. 'Hey ...'

'What is it?' For a moment Aunt Addie looked alarmed.

'Something's down there. An eel maybe. Or a snake.'

Aunt Addie laughed. It was a bit like a horse laughing, thought Harry. Maybe if you lived with a unicorn you started to sound a bit like one, too.

'That be the water sprite.'

'The what? But they're just in books!'

'You read books? It's good to read books,' said Aunt Addie. 'Once I read books all the time. I have no books here though.'

'Maybe I could bring you some,' offered Harry.

Aunt Addie seemed to consider. Then she shook her head. 'They may not be the same,' she said finally. 'It's better not.'

'But why not?' began Harry. He stopped. There was something about Aunt Addie that stopped you asking questions. As though what Aunt Addie decided simply was.

'Dad said you needed something,' said Harry finally. 'But he didn't tell me what. Do you need a hand with something? I'm strong for my age,' he offered. 'Do you need firewood? Or something nailed up? I made a new chook house these holidays.'

'Chook house?' asked Aunt Addie doubtfully.

'Yeah, you know. Chooks. Hens,' said Harry.

'Ah, hens,' said Aunt Addie. She seemed to choke down a smile. 'I have no hens here.'

'No chooks? What do you do for eggs then?'

'My friends bring me what I need,' said Aunt Addie. 'And I grow what they need in return.'

'Friends?' Harry blinked doubtfully. What friends would she have up here? 'What things do you grow?' he asked politely.

Aunt Addie's smile was as bright as the tall golden flowers. 'Divers things,' she offered. She gestured at a spire edged with cup-shaped red flowers. 'Hollyhocks for them to drink from. And foxgloves for them to sleep in. And fairies' fishing rods to fish with, and clover for their ale.'

'Hold on a sec,' said Harry. 'What are you talking about? Foxgloves to sleep in? What are foxgloves?'

Aunt Addie gestured at some tall pale pinkish purple flowers. 'These are foxgloves,' she said.

'To sleep on? You mean they dry them and make mattresses from them …'

'They sleep in the flowers!' laughed Aunt Addie.

'They what? But no one can sleep in flowers.'

'Fairies do,' said Aunt Addie.

Fairies! For a moment Harry thought she meant something else … but she didn't, he realised. She meant real fairies. 'Fairies with wings and wands?' he asked cautiously.

'Sometimes,' said Aunt Addie matter-of-factly. 'Betimes they bring their wands.'

She was barmy. She had to be. Thinking she had fairies in her garden and water sprites …

The unicorn snickered from the grassy bank and tossed its bright horn at the sky.

… and unicorns. She really did have a unicorn. This was *real*, really real.

'Do the fairies come often?' he asked hesitantly.

Aunt Addie looked amused. 'They're here all the time,' she said. 'Look! You see! There they are!'

Something fluttered round the spire of a — what had Aunt Addie called them? Hollyhocks. But it was just a bee. A bee with shimmering wings that glistened blue and silver as they caught the sun.

Harry blinked. The glistening thing was gone.

Aunt Addie's smile was serene, as though of course he'd seen the fairy, as though unicorns and water sprites were perfectly natural, just like a garden like this was something you saw every day, too. She looked at him consideringly. 'Belike you *can* help me.'

Harry nodded. 'Sure. How?'

'You can help me pick the raspberries.' Aunt Addie lifted her skirts a little as she brushed past the flowers down the path. Harry followed her uncertainly.

'Raspberries? I'm not sure. I mean …'

'You've never picked raspberries? For shame.'

'I don't think they'd grow down at our place,' said Harry.

'There's no skill to picking raspberries,' said Aunt Addie kindly. 'You pick them and you eat them, and what don't be eaten you put in the basket. You line the basket with leaves first. Raspberries are easily bruised.'

'I guess they would be,' said Harry. 'I mean I have eaten them. You can buy them frozen at the supermarket in town.'

'The supermarket?' said Aunt Addie vaguely. She picked a basket off a branch as they passed under the trees. It was a funny looking basket, thought Harry, a bit lopsided. It looked like it was made of twisted branches instead of cane.

Aunt Addie reached up and picked the broad green leaves. 'Soft leaves,' she said to Harry. 'See how soft they are?'

Harry nodded.

'Leaves should be soft,' said Aunt Addie dreamily. 'Soft and browning when they fall. Don't you love the leaves when they fall?'

'Er …' said Harry.

'Raspberries,' said Aunt Addie more matter-of-factly. 'You take that side and I'll take this. Don't be ashamed of eating them neither. That's what raspberries are for.'

The raspberries were hot and squishy sweet. It was hard to stop eating them once you started, thought Harry guiltily, as he forced himself to lay some in the basket. After all he was here to help Aunt Addie. That's what Dad had said. Aunt Addie needed something.

Surely not just help picking the raspberries.

'Tell me then,' said Aunt Addie after a while. 'Tell me about Ron. It's so strange, thinking of him as your father. Little Ron a father, too. Tell me about him.'

'Er … there's not much to tell,' said Harry. What was there to say about Dad?

'What does he look like now?' asked Aunt Addie.

'Well, he's tall.'

'He would be tall,' said Aunt Addie approvingly. 'He were tall enough back then.'

'And he farms our place.'

Aunt Addie's face clouded just a little. 'Ah yes, the farm,' she said. She shook her head. 'Tell me other things,' she said. 'He married. Who is your dear mother then?'

'Mum? She's just Mum. She works part time at the library in town. That's how Dad met her. She was new to town …' It all seemed far away from the flowers and the clearing. 'Hey, do you really want to hear all this?'

Aunt Addie nodded solemnly. 'I want to hear,' she said. 'Sometimes I'm afeared …'

Afeared? 'Afraid? Afraid of what, Aunt Addie?'
Unicorns, fairies, water sprites. Maybe there were
dragons, too … or wizards.

But Aunt Addie was laughing. 'Of nothing surely.
Bless your sweet face, what is there to be afeared of
here? I'm silly sometimes, that's all. I think … but
enough of that. Would you like a nuncheon?'

'A nuncheon?'

'Vittles, food. You must be hungry,' said Aunt Addie
gently. 'Walking all that way. I'm grateful. You must tell
your father so.'

'Yes, I'll tell him. Yes, I'd love something to eat,' said
Harry before he thought about it. Crikey, what
would she give him to eat then? Fairy bread or
elves' porridge …

Aunt Addie took the basket, half-filled with
raspberries now, and floated up the path again. She
gestured to the seat among the flowers. Again she didn't
ask him in. Why not? thought Harry. But it didn't
matter. It was beautiful here in the sun. Beautiful, that
was the only word for it. As though the whole world
was beauty.

He opened his eyes at the sound of Aunt Addie's step
on the path. She wore funny shoes, he noticed, sort of
slippers, shining and in bright colours, almost like they
were made of silk.

She carried a tray filled with more of the peaches, and apples too and cherries, and some funny nuts, and some sort of bun thing and honeycomb in a blue bowl.

'They're hazelnuts,' said Aunt Addie, as he picked one up curiously. 'Your father didn't know hazelnuts either. They're plentiful up here. And that's acorn bread. The baby fairies sleep in acorn cradles and the bees rock them in the wind.'

The bird sang again, that strange sweet bird. The song twisted in his brain and carried it along. It wouldn't be so bad living up here, thought Harry. All the fruit you wanted and green grass all year round — somehow he knew this grass never dried off no matter how hot the summer. You could swim in the pool with the water sprite and the fairies would keep you company.

He tried to jerk his mind back to reality. But there were no fairies. Of course there were no fairies.

'Aunt Addie?' he said almost desperately. 'What was it you wanted me to do? The thing Dad said you needed?'

Aunt Addie's smile seemed far away. 'You brang it when you came,' she said. 'I have it here. I'll keep it safe.'

'But what was it? What do you mean?'

'Sleep,' said Aunt Addie's voice. 'It is a long walk back. Just sleep. Just sleep.'

The bird sang again. Harry shut his eyes. His dreams were filled with unicorns and silver wings and the liquid singing of the bird. And then a sheep called somewhere on the hill. A dog barked in reply. The dreams changed, and Harry dreamt of home.

The farmhouse crouched between the sheds. There was no light in the kitchen. Mum must be reading in bed.

The old sofa creaked on the verandah. Dad looked out through the darkness.

Harry said nothing as he climbed the steps.

'So, you found her,' said Dad softly.

Harry nodded. 'How did you know?'

'By your face. I felt like that, too, when I first met Aunt Addie.'

'It was real, wasn't it?' asked Harry. 'All of it was real?'

'It was real,' said Dad. 'Real enough, at any rate. Real enough to see and smell and hear.'

'Who is she, Dad?'

Dad moved over on the sofa. Harry sat next to him. The cushions felt stiff. Too much possum, Mum had said, though she'd tried to wash it out.

'I told you,' said Dad. 'Your great-something-aunt.'

'Go on,' said Harry.

Dad sighed. 'I only know what my dad told me. What

his dad told him too. It's a long story. Sure you're not too tired?'

'Go on,' said Harry again.

'No, you wouldn't be too tired,' said Dad. 'I remember the first time I went to Aunt Addie's ... Anyway, it all started with your great-great-something-granddad. He settled here in the 1840s.

'It was all bush then. No paddocks. Just the trees. It was wild and isolated but he loved it. He married your great-something-gran, and she loved it, too. She was the daughter of a farmer up past Black Stone Creek. She'd been born there. It never occurred to her that someone mightn't love it, too.'

'Where does Aunt Addie fit in?'

'I'm coming to that,' said Dad.

'Aunt Addie was your great-something-granddad's younger sister. Twenty years younger — it happened a lot back then, a gap as big as that. Families had lots of kids in those days. They were farm kids, too, almost as isolated as this probably, but different country. Very different country. Addie was only five when your great-something-granddad left to come to Australia, but she loved him, and she remembered him.

'They wrote to each other — though remember in those days it took a letter six months or so to cross the ocean. He told her about his farm, his lovely, lovely farm, about his wife, his sweet, sweet wife. They're the words Dad used to me, and his dad to him, all the way back. His lovely, lovely farm, his sweet, sweet wife.

'Then something happened to Aunt Addie. I don't know what it was. Dad just said his dad told him she'd been crossed in love. That's how they put it back in the last century.

'I don't know what it was all about. Maybe she was engaged to some bloke who ran off on her. Maybe she fell in love with someone her parents didn't like. Those sorts of things happened in those days. You had to marry someone your parents approved of.

'Who knows. But she was unhappy and she wrote to her brother, and he said, "Come out here. There's plenty of room on the farm." I suppose he thought there were many more men than women in the colony, too, she's sure to get a husband here.

'So he wrote to her, and she wrote back, and the next year she came.'

A dog muttered in its sleep down at the kennels. 'Go on,' said Harry.

'It was a long voyage out, but she was happy. It must have all been strange to a girl from the backcountry like she was, who'd never even been to a city before. But she was full of hope. She was going to a new land, a new farm, going to her beloved brother, her older brother she hadn't seen for nearly fifteen years.

'She landed at Sydney. Her brother was shearing and couldn't meet her, but he arranged for her to be met, taken to a respectable boarding house and put on the coach next morning.

'He met her up in town. He shaved specially — in those days men shaved maybe once a week. But it'd been a long shearing. His hair was shaggy. His face was brown. He wasn't the brother she remembered.

'He brought her home. His wife had made Johnny cakes and they ate them on the verandah, right where we're sitting now, though the rest of the house wasn't built back then, just this front bit with a sort of separate kitchen out the back. The flies sat on the Johnny cakes and got stuck in the treacle. And Aunt Addie sat on the verandah horrified at what she'd come to.

'Aunt Addie stuck it out, even though they killed a snake the first morning she was here, and she was scared to go down to the dunny ever after.

'She was scared of the snakes, of the bunyip howling down the creek, of the wind that tore down the hills and the heat that sent the branches cracking off the trees. She was scared of the smoke from the bushfires in the distance. But she stuck it out.'

'Did she fall in love again?' asked Harry.

Dad shook his head. 'There were men around. Stockmen, farmers, shopkeepers up in town. Every woman in the colony had a string of suitors in those days. But she didn't fall in love again.

'She was homesick. She missed the trees, the soft green trees. She missed the bluebells in the spring. She missed the roses over the fence at home. She missed the sound of bees in the spring blossom.'

'Why didn't she go home then?' asked Harry.

'It was a long way remember,' said Dad. 'Expensive, too. And when she got back she'd just be an old maid, unwanted … and her parents were getting older and what would happen when they died? There were so few jobs for women in those days. Be someone's servant or nurse … I doubt she had the education for governess. You know how she talks … There was nothing for her at home, except the forests and the gardens that she loved. She'd sit here on the verandah and look out at the hills and she'd remember the flowers and the stories of home.

'So her brother decided they'd plant a garden for her here, something to remind her of the world she loved. She brightened up when he told her about that.

'Your great-something-grandfather wrote to Sydney and ordered plants from there. He got English catalogues and had plants and seeds sent out — a long journey for them too remember.'

'And the garden grew?' asked Harry, looking out at Mum's tubs of petunias by the steps, the grevilleas by the front gate, the rockery where the dogs liked to sleep.

'No.' Dad looked out at the hills again. 'Most of the bulbs didn't even come up — either it was too hot or they'd been damaged in the ship or they never did get used to the change in seasons. The roses died — I reckon we've got hardier sorts now that've got used to Australia. The lily shoots shrivelled in the ground. She couldn't even get a lawn to grow. They didn't have hoses in those days, remember, or sprinkler systems. Gardens needed the rain or they died. And Aunt Addie's died.

'Aunt Addie didn't say anything. She didn't say much at all by then. Then one morning she was gone.

'Your great-something-granddad panicked. He thought she'd been bitten by a snake, drowned in the waterhole. All the blokes went looking — then that evening she turned up, cool as you please. She hadn't been bitten by a snake. She hadn't even got lost.'

'Where had she been?'

'Up at the hut. The one where she lives now. In those days it was just a shepherd's hut — a place to check the sheep when they were up that way — but it hadn't been used since the main house was built.

'Aunt Addie asked if she could grow a garden there. It was cooler up in the hills she reckoned. She'd get water from the creek in the gully.

'Of course your great-granddad said yes. Anything to make her smile again. She spent the next year digging up the shrivelled bulbs from round the house, carefully separating the lilies from the hot soil, uprooting the roses in case there was still a spark of life.

'Years went by. Sometimes she asked her brother for seeds — grass seeds, forget-me-not seeds, hollyhock seeds. But mostly she just wandered up there in the early morning and came back late at night. Finally your great-something-granddad stopped worrying about her. She knew the way. She always came back safely.

'More years went by. Your great-something-granddad had kids — your ancestor and a few others, too. Aunt Addie told the kids stories about "home" — the beech trees dappled against the sky, the fairies and the unicorns. I reckon by that time she didn't know what "home" was really like — memories of her childhood were all mixed with her stories and ... well, who knows with what else.

'She spent more and more time up at the hut.'

'Didn't anyone ever go up to see what she was doing there?' asked Harry.

Dad shook his head. 'She asked them not to. She said they could see it when it was done. Her brother and sister-in-law did what she asked. I reckon they thought that garden was probably dead, too and Addie just wouldn't admit it, would keep on hoping that one day things would grow.'

'But surely some of the stockmen would have passed by!' objected Harry.

'You'd think so,' said Dad. 'You'd think someone would have come by. But they didn't. We can probably guess why.

'Then one day ... the first of May it was, just like today, her nephew thought he'd follow her.' Dad's voice died away. A possum shrieked out in the gum tree by the shed, and then was still.

'What happened then?' asked Harry.

'What happened to you, I reckon,' said Dad. 'What happened to me and my dad and my granddad, too. He met Aunt Addie. And he saw her garden.

'Aunt Addie didn't come back to the farm that night. She never came back again. For years her brother tried to find her hut. But the only one who ever did was her nephew. Every May Day he went up there. Just like me. Now just like you.'

'But … but you don't go there anymore,' said Harry. 'Did you have an argument? Did she ask you not to come?'

His father shook his head. 'No argument. Just one May Day I couldn't find it anymore. I hunted for hours. I was sure I'd gone the wrong way, gone up the wrong gully — but deep inside I knew what had happened.'

'I … I don't understand …'

'I had grown up. Aunt Addie didn't want me in her garden anymore. Not with the unicorn, the water sprite, the fairies — didn't you see the fairies, too?'

'I think I did,' said Harry.

'That's all that ever happens,' said Dad. 'You think you might have seen … Grown ups don't fit into the world of fairies. And no man can ride the unicorn.'

'Then one day I won't be able to find Aunt Addie's either,' said Harry slowly.

'One day,' said his father. 'In a few years' time. Then one day you'll have to tell your son how he can find Aunt Addie's.'

'Dad?'

'Mmmm?' His father's eyes were on the moon, round as a golden hill, emerging from the black behind the ridge.

'Did Aunt Addie ever ask you into her house?'

'No,' said Dad.

'Why not?'

His father grinned. 'What maiden lady of last century would ask a gentleman into her bedroom? Even one as young as you.'

'Oh,' said Harry. 'I thought it might break the spell.'

'I don't think so,' said his father gently. 'I don't think the spell can be broken now.'

'You know,' said Harry after a while. 'I almost stayed there. It was so beautiful. So strange. I thought I could never leave.'

'Then you remembered home,' said his father.

'How did you know?' asked Harry.

'Because it happened to me, too,' said his father. 'Just like that. I remembered the sun on the hills and the sheep by the rocks. And I came home.'

Home, thought Harry. The bare gold hills like skulls, their shape all clean and clear under the dead grass. The hot haze of eucalypt oil around the trees that made the distance blue. The sunlight baking on corrugated iron. The hunched backs of rocks in the paddocks …

'What was it Aunt Addie needed?' asked Harry.

'Haven't you guessed?'

Harry shook his head.

'Maybe you will next time,' said his father. 'It took me a while, too.'

'Not fair,' said Harry. 'Tell me now, Dad.'

His father shrugged. 'Reality,' he said. 'That's what she needs from us. A little bit of reality to ground that world of hers. A little bit of something that's not memories and dreams. Otherwise … who knows …'

The clearing had shimmered when he'd first seen it, Harry remembered. And by the time he left the shapes and colours were clear …

'Do you think she's lonely?' asked Harry finally.

'No,' said Dad. 'She's got her unicorn, her water sprite and her fairies. I reckon she'd say we were the lonely ones. But we're not. There's another sort of magic here that Addie never learnt to see. Come on. Your mum will be waiting. It's time we went inside.'

Amfylobbsis

he hospital bed was cool, the sheets were straight and firm. You didn't need eyes to tell it was a hospital, Grandma decided. The smells, the sounds, the very feel of the air conditioning on your skin was enough to tell you where you were.

'Grandma?' The voice at the door was eager. 'Have they taken the bandages off yet?'

'Emma, is that you, pet? No, tomorrow. They'll take the bandages off tomorrow.'

'But we'll be gone tomorrow!' The voice came nearer. 'Can I come in?'

'Of course.'

'Can Amfylobbsis come in, too?'

Grandma smiled. 'I'd love to see Amfylobbsis.'

'But you can't see,' Emma pointed out. 'You won't be able to see until tomorrow.'

'Not even then, pet,' said Grandma gently. 'It'll take weeks for my eyes to get better.'

'But you'll be able to see again properly? Really properly?'

'Of course,' said Grandma.

I hope, she thought. Why do we always lie to children? Why do we always tell them everything will be all right?

'Is Amfylobbsis here yet?' she asked aloud.

Emma giggled. 'No. He had to hide from the nurses.

They might be angry if they find him in their hospital.'

'But no one ever sees Amfylobbsis except you.'

'They might hear him though,' said Emma seriously. Something clattered outside — a trolley perhaps, thought Grandma. 'He's here now,' said Emma. 'Say hello to Grandma, Amfylobbsis.' She paused. 'Amfylobbsis says to say hello.'

'Hello, Amfylobbsis,' said Grandma.

Emma was silent for a moment. 'You're the only one who believes in Amfylobbsis except me,' she said finally. 'Everyone else says he's just imaginary. I'll miss you when we're in Darwin, Grandma.'

'I'll miss you too, pet,' said Grandma. 'And Amfylobbsis,' she added. 'But we'll see each other often.'

'Promise?'

'Promise,' said Grandma. She tried to sound convincing. Darwin was so far away ...

Emma was silent.

'Emma, what does Amfylobbsis look like? Is he big?'

'Really big,' said Emma. 'Almost as tall as me.'

Grandma smiled. 'It must be hard for him to hide so no one sees him then.'

'Amfylobbsis says he's had lots of practice hiding,' said Emma matter-of-factly.

'Is he a boy? Or a dog? Or a monster? Or ...?'

'Of course he's not a monster. He's sort of like a horse,'

said Emma. 'Like a white horse. But he's different. Like a fairy horse maybe.'

'Has he got wings?'

'No.' Emma sounded regretful. 'Just this big horn thing in the middle of his head. It's sharp. I was scared of it at first but Amfylobbsis said …'

'Then he's a unicorn!' said Grandma.

'Is that what he is?' said Emma excitedly. 'I didn't know. Have you seen unicorns before, Grandma?'

'No, they're …' She was about to say they were imaginary. She stopped. 'They're pretty rare,' she said instead.

The nurse's voice came from the doorway. 'Visiting hours are nearly over,' she said.

Emma sat quite still. 'I don't want to go,' she whispered.

'I'll see you before you leave tomorrow.'

'But everyone will be there then. It's not the same. It's hard to bring Amfylobbsis when there's so many people.'

'We'll still see each other often, pet,' said Grandma, this time to try to convince herself. If only things were different, she thought suddenly. If only this was the sort of world where hopes came true, where small girls did play with unicorns.

'Grandma?'

'Yes?'

'Amfylobbsis just said not to worry. He said everything will work out fine.'

'Thank you, Amfylobbsis,' said Grandma gently.

'He'd like to say goodbye now.'

'Goodbye Amfylobbsis,' said Grandma.

'No, goodbye properly,' said Emma. 'Because you're the only one who believes in him except me. Because he loves you, too.'

Grandma smiled. 'How do I say goodbye properly?'

'Hold out your hand,' whispered Emma.

Grandma held out her hand.

Nothing happened. She half expected Emma to put a lollie in it … a jube, maybe, she and Emma both loved jubes. Then suddenly …

The touch was gentle, moist and very warm. The hint of hot breath, the touch of whiskers round a soft damp mouth …

'Goodbye, Grandma,' whispered Emma.

Grandma listened to her footsteps run along the corridor, and faintly, very faintly, the light clicking of hooves.

Spots

The room smelt of sweat and old bedding. The child sat in the corner, spooning soup.

'It's a miracle,' the woman said. 'A true miracle.'

The girl shook her head. Her face was pale and thin, but not too thin. The illness had been too brief to really mark her face.

'I knew I would get better,' she said. 'The girl came.'

'What girl?'

'The girl with the unicorn,' said the child matter-of-factly. 'When she comes you get better. Everyone knows that.'

The woman shook her head. 'There are signs and portents everywhere,' she said quietly. 'They say that when the plague comes to a village the first sign is a tall man carrying an axe, his head cloaked, and shining evil eyes. No one who's seen him has ever lived to tell the tale ...'

'Then how do people know about him?' asked the child. 'I didn't see a man, though others say they did. But all of us saw the girl.'

'No one really sees him,' said the woman. 'You just had a fever dream. That's what it was. But you're better now, and soon we'll be taking you home ...'

'But I did see her!' insisted the child. 'She was young and had long hair, and she was dressed all in white and the unicorn was white as well.'

'A unicorn was it? Well, that proves it was a dream.'

'I did see her,' said the child stubbornly, laying down her spoon. Tears ran down her cheeks suddenly. 'She came riding up the path and her cloak was white and the unicorn had big blue eyes and she carried a basket. But she came too late for Ma and Da ...'

'Well, yes,' said the woman comfortingly. 'If that's what you saw, well, that's what you saw. You'll be home with us and you'll forget it all soon. There'll be kittens for you to play with and your cousins to play with too and ...'

'But I don't want to forget the unicorn!' cried the child. 'It put its face through the window and blew through its lips at me. And the girl came inside and felt my forehead and her hand was cool, so cool. And she took a sweetie out of her basket, a little white one and she made me swallow it. Then she took Ma and Da outside.'

'Sure and sure she did,' soothed the woman. 'Or maybe it was the neighbours took them.'

'No one would touch the dead!' said the child. 'Not till the girl came on the unicorn! She gave the sweeties to everyone, two every day, and no one died after that. And she gave us water — funny sweet water and strange cakes to eat, and ...'

The woman leant over the child and wrapped another shawl around her. 'And here's your uncle with the cart,' she said. 'It's time to take you home. Your new home.'

The child nodded. 'I was asleep the last time she came,' she said. 'I just remember her pushing the last sweetie in my mouth, then I fell asleep again. So I never said goodbye. Or thank you.' She looked up at her aunt. 'Do you think if I said goodbye now she'd hear me?'

'I'm sure of it,' said her aunt, for after all it was no lie. Dreams could hear you anywhere.

'Thank you,' said the child earnestly, gazing out the door as though she expected the unicorn to appear again. 'Thank you for looking after me. Thank you for making me well. And thank Spots, too.'

'Spots?' asked the woman.

'That's what she called the unicorn,' said the child.

'But I thought it was a white unicorn!' protested the woman.

'It was,' said the child sleepily. 'But it was still called Spots.'

She lifted up her arms to be carried.

Ten minutes away, a thousand years away, another world away, the girl got off the unicorn and led it tiredly into its stable. It snickered at the horse in the next stall, then bent its head to its hay.

'Hard time?' said a voice behind the girl.

The girl turned. 'Oh, it's you,' she said. 'It's always hard. Sometimes …'

'Sometimes what?'

'Sometimes I wonder if it's right. To interfere. To pretend to all those people.' She patted the unicorn absently.

'We have to pretend,' said her friend. 'What would people like that say if we came just like we are? They'd be terrified. No, it has to be this way. Disguised as the sort of visions they dreamt about in those days … and the unicorn was a touch of genius. Whoever thought of the unicorn?'

'Thaddeus,' said the girl. 'It was Thaddeus, of course. Just a little fiddle with the DNA he said, and there we had a unicorn. Though it was spotty, not pure white, something went wrong there, but nothing that some hair dye wouldn't change. And its blue eyes. The blue eyes were a shock to Thaddeus, too. No one quite knows where the blue eyes came from.'

The unicorn blew gently at its hay for a moment, almost as though it was laughing.

'You know, it's funny.'

'What?'

'The last village I was in and the one before — they said they'd seen another vision.'

'Another unicorn? Maybe it's a story passed about from some other village you went to.'

The girl shook her head. 'A tall man with an axe. Before the plague arrives, they said. Every time, the man appears.'

Her friend was silent. 'Who knows where the plague came from?' she said. 'All we know is why it stops. Because of us. Because of antibiotics disguised as sweeties. Because of the unicorn.'

The girl smiled suddenly. 'We're a match for anyone, aren't we, Spots?' She patted the rough back. 'You know, sometimes I wonder if you're not magic after all. Real magic.'

Her friend laughed. 'Don't let Thaddeus hear you say that. You'd be in for a long lecture. Come on. We've waited dinner for you.'

The girl patted the unicorn one last time. 'See you tomorrow, Spots,' she said.

The unicorn winked at her with one blue eye.

The Taming of the Beast

he beast had pale skin, paler than she'd ever seen before. It hovered nervously at the edge of the clearing.

It was scared. Even from here she could see that it was scared.

She started to speak to it; then stopped. Of course it wouldn't understand. One animal never understood another's words. Each creature had its own language and that was how it always was … it was the tone of the words that animals understood, the music behind the words …

The beast hesitated. Was it going to run? It had been plucking apples, she noticed. One lay on the ground where it had fallen, still with the imprint of the beast's sharp teeth.

She stepped forward quietly. One harsh move and the beast would vanish. What sort of creature was it? She'd never seen its like before. A strange beast. An almost frightening beast. But there was something about it that called her to it. As though they belonged together, as though once they'd been a partnership, or would be friends …

Another step. The beast looked wary, but it held its ground. A brave beast, she thought exultantly. A good creature for a friend.

Another step. Another. Now the beast stepped forward, too, the long hair down its neck shaking a little as it trembled. But it still came on …

She could smell the beast now, a strange smell, deep and warmly musky.

One more step. Slowly … very slowly … she reached towards the creature.

The beast flinched, then smiled. She knew it was a smile. Who would have thought a beast like that would smile, too? The smile looked different, that funny mouth, those crazy teeth. But still she knew it was a smile.

Slowly … very slowly … the beast reached towards her, too.

Its skin was warm, and smoother than she'd thought. What now? What now?

Suddenly it was simple. As though not only were they meant to be together but she knew how … and the creature knew it, too.

The beast laughed and she laughed too, and though their laughter was different each understood.

Then she was galloping, galloping through the shadows of the leaves, with the beast clinging to her back, its two long legs on either side, its face bent low so the long hair on its head tangled her mane and fluttered up towards her horn.

The wind tore away their laughter and mingled it and sent it flying through the trees.

The Lady
of
The Unicorn

he hill was steep, the grass a strange unearthly green. The unicorn picked his way uncertainly among the bones and rubble. His hooves looked very white among the green. His flanks were wet with sweat when Ethel patted them.

The hill stank too, thought Ethel, as she clung to the unicorn's mane. This wasn't the Hall's familiar smell of chamber pots and dogs and winter sweat. This was a sharper smell, of bones withering in sunlight, of hot rock and decomposing flesh ... and something else ...

The unicorn dodged around a chunk of rubble, worn smooth by rain and wind till it almost looked natural, higher than Ethel's head even when she was riding. At least the piles of rubble shielded her from sight if anyone looked down.

But of course no one was looking down. No one lived on the hill. The giant on the hill was just a tale of M'um Margot's to frighten children if they yelled too loudly in the Hall. It was just a trick of Uncle Maddox's in the days when he could tell her what to do. Don't go to the forest you'll be eaten by a dragon, don't climb the wild hills or a lion will tear off both your arms.

Don't climb up the hill or the giant will suck your bones ...

Giants were olden day myths, Ethel thought, like werewolves and koalas and dragons. No one she knew had ever really seen a werewolf or even a giant, though M'um Dorothy the Baker had seen a lion when she was young.

But lions were real. The old books agreed that lions were real, just like sheep and goats had once been real before they interbred as geep. There'd been lion parks in the old days, then in the wild days the lions had escaped. But werewolves and giants and dragons and monsters were all imaginary. The old books said they were.

The unicorn stumbled, then righted himself. Ethel glanced down at a large bone, a thigh bone from a cow maybe or from a horse. Who would eat a horse? A giant maybe or a ...

There were no such things as giants.

The bone was splintered at one end, as though it had been crunched in giant jaws. A few bits of meat clung to the other end. Raw meat, rancid and festering in the sun. A fly buzzed, slow and sleepy, then settled back onto the meat.

Ethel hesitated. Many things might carry away a bone ... foxes, eagles ... Just because there was a bone didn't mean there was a giant.

Would a fox or an eagle splinter a bone like that?

The bone had been baking at least two days. Whatever had crunched it was probably long gone. Ethel patted the unicorn again to tell him to keep climbing. The unicorn stumbled again. Ethel dismounted and began to lead him.

Round a hunk of concrete, crowned with twisted steel, then round another. A snake slithered slowly into a crevice, its belly red against the sandy stone. The grass was soft and still, and that strange and brilliant green. Maybe grass just grew well between the rocks. Maybe the giant cast a spell …

There were no such thing as spells either, Ethel told herself firmly.

The stench grew stronger instead of weaker. High above a pair of crows yelled into silence.

Surely she must be nearly at the top. But the piles of rubble stood too high, with chunks of concrete, fat as Ned the Barrel Maker. It was impossible to see above them to see how far she had to climb.

The unicorn whinnied softly, distressed by the stench. Ethel shivered. What if the giant heard it — though of course there was no giant. But there was no need to take the unicorn further either. She'd be faster, quieter on foot.

Ethel assessed the rubble quickly. Surely there must be a place to tie the reins. There were no trees, no bushes, the steel was all too rusty, it would never hold … But there must be something …

Finally she chose a cow's skull, wedged firmly between great hunks of stone. She slipped the reins around the horns, then patted the unicorn, murmuring to him in the no-words language that they shared. The unicorn butted her shoulder with his warm white nose. The whites of his eyes were showing around the clear soft blue of the iris. His ears were narrow and pointed. They twitched towards the top of the hill as though listening to sounds that Ethel couldn't hear.

'I won't be long,' whispered Ethel, hoping that the unicorn understood the tone if not the words. 'You'll be safe here.'

She hoped that she was right.

Up the hill, twisting between the rubble, through the too-green grass. Suddenly the rubble cleared. The top of the hill opened in front of her.

Ethel gasped, she closed her mouth, afraid that she'd been heard.

Once the top of the hill must have been bare as Uncle Maddox's head, a grassy clearing grazed perhaps by nimble geep. Now it was divided neatly into gardens, each edged by jagged rocks, as though the chunks of rubble from below had been split and shattered. Fruit trees clustered against sun-warm walls.

A mound of even larger chunks of rubble clustered in the centre of the clearing. Ethel blinked and saw it was a hut.

A strange hut, a massive hut, more like a cave than any hut should be, but built by human hands none the less. Tree trunks poked out above thick walls, roofed with long thin slabs, like shingles that someone had turned to stone. The hut would just look like a pile of rubble from a distance, thought Ethel. You'd never know a hut was here from below.

Now she was closer she could see smoke as well. It came from the far side of the hut — clear, hot smoke from long dry wood, so the air merely shimmered instead of clouded grey.

The stench was even worse.

She should run. She had to run. She had to get her feet to work. M'um Margot was right. Even Uncle had been right.

She had to run …

Suddenly her feet began to move. Down between the rubble, to the right and to the right again, never mind the easiest way now, just the quickest to get down, to get away, down to her unicorn and home.

'Aaaaah!' Ethel bit the sound back. Something gripped her foot. A snare of plaited leather grew tighter as she pulled.

Ethel froze. She mustn't make a noise. She mustn't panic. She wasn't a wallaby or wild geep to be caught blindly with a bit of leather. She only had to stop and wriggle her foot free … but even as she thought it she realised that it made no difference what noise she made. A bell was ringing high up on the hill.

The snare must have set off an alarm.

It was a dull bell, not like the sharp tuneful bells at home, more like a clapper against a ring of steel than a proper bell cast in a forge, all its proportions right to sing its note. But this wasn't a singing bell, or a bell to call you in from the fields. This was a hunter's bell, a command to come and fetch your prey.

Ethel tore urgently at her foot. A wild dog might bite through the snare. Her teeth weren't as sharp as a wild dog's teeth, but maybe she could manage it — but not in time, not in time. Maybe if she pointed her toes downward her foot would be narrower and might slip out. Yes, that was it. She took her slipper off. But the snare stuck around her heel and held it firm.

A noise came from above. Like a crow learning to sing, thought Ethel with half her mind. She struggled frantically, but knew it was too late.

Footsteps. Heavy footsteps. A chunk of rubble rolled as something large brushed against it — *ca-thunk, ca-thunk, ca-thunk* down the hill, till it crashed against another and was still.

The booming sound came closer.

'*And he sang as he stuffed that jumbuck in his tucker bag …*'

Ethel froze. It was a song from the olden days. She'd read it in a book in the Hall. One of her greatest joys at the Hall was the big room full of books. There'd been music written for this song too, but no one at the Hall could play it …

The giant stepped around the boulder.

It was small for a giant, was her first thought. She'd always thought that giants would be much bigger. Though this was big enough.

The giant was no taller than two men, though its arms and legs were slightly longer in proportion, so the hands hung down below the knees.

It was cleaner than Ethel had expected too, the long hair plaited neatly and wound about its head. Its head was bare. Ethel had thought only the T'manians had bare heads. Perhaps neither they nor giants ever got the sun sickness. It wore a shapeless tunic, like faded dark green curtains, belted roughly several times with a leather thong below its breasts and sewn roughly at the shoulders and down part of the side so that its lower legs gleamed long and bare and hairy.

The giant was definitely a woman.

The giant stopped singing. She blinked at Ethel. Her eyes were just a little larger than they should be too. And then she grinned.

'A mouse,' she boomed. 'A little mousie! How are we meant to dine upon a mousie then? There's not much meat upon a mousie.' Her teeth were whiter than any Ethel had ever seen, and longer than they should be. It looked like she still had all of them, though she must be M'um Margot's age or more.

The giant lifted her great hands, wide as pitchforks, brown as any field hands, though the nails were clean. 'Maybe I'll have the little mousie stewed, or fried. It be most tender boiled inside my pot ...'

The giant cackled. It bent down and snapped the thongs that bound her ankle. The giant stood back. 'I will cook the little mousie and suck her bones. I will hang her like a wombat in my larder till she be soft. She'll be a delicate little morsel for such as me.' The giant blinked and folded her arms. 'For mercy's sake, why aren't you running girl?' the giant said in a normal voice.

'I don't know,' said Ethel truthfully.

'Look child, if a giant catches you in her snare and talks about turning your bones into soup, it's prudent to run, run as fast as you can, then tell everyone about your narrow escape. You understand me?'

'Yes,' said Ethel.

'Well, go on then. Scamper.'

Ethel shook her head.

'Stubborn,' grinned the giant, showing her too-white, too-long teeth. 'Stubborn as … well, I know of only one thing as stubborn and that's me, so I suppose I shouldn't complain. What am I to do with you if you don't run?'

'Turn me into soup?' offered Ethel.

'Don't joke about it child, it's no joking matter. I only have two options up on my hill. I can hurt people or I can scare them, and big as I am, I can't defend this place myself if a whole mob came at me. So I'm left with scaring people. Sensible people, who allow themselves to be scared.'

'I was scared,' objected Ethel.

'But you still didn't run. Why didn't you run?' inquired the giant, as though she really wanted to know. 'Maybe I can improve my performance next time.'

'Because I was more interested than scared,' decided Ethel.

The giant leant against a chunk of weathered concrete, her wide hands almost dropping against the ground. Her fingers were broader at the tips than below, like fattish spoons, thought Ethel.

'So,' remarked the giant. 'Scared but not running. Curious. Lonely perhaps? So lonely you would dare even a giant?'

'I'm not lonely,' objected Ethel. 'I'm the Lady of the Unicorn.' She waited for the giant's face to change.

The giant looked unimpressed.

'Don't you know who the Lady of the Unicorn is?' demanded Ethel.

'More or less,' said the giant. 'I've never been much interested in who is what in the villages down below my hill. How did you become the Lady? Was there a competition?'

Ethel shook her head. 'When the old Lady died, they sent out searchers to find a new unicorn because hers wouldn't go to anyone else, of course. And when they found one they took it to the Hall, and sent it out to find an owner.'

'And it found you?'

Ethel nodded. 'I was up a tree picking apples. The unicorn stopped under my branch. I threw him an apple. He looked hungry ... and sort of lonely. I didn't know they were choosing a new Lady. I just thought — I don't know what I thought. And so I slid down the tree and the unicorn butted my arms for more apples, so I fed him more, even though Uncle Maddox would be angry. And then, and then ... I sort of slid onto his back. I don't know why I did that either. And suddenly these six old men and women were racing up to us and they bowed and called me "my Lady" and they've called me "my Lady" ever since.'

'What about your parents?'

Ethel shrugged. 'I don't remember them. The T'manians killed them down south in a raid when I was small. I moved up here with Uncle Maddox and my cousins; but there were a lot of cousins and I was just a nuisance. They made a great fuss of me of course when I became the Lady — I think they thought I'd have them at the Hall. Or give them presents. But why should I? They didn't want me when I was just Ethel. Why should I want them when I became the Lady?'

'No reason that I can think of,' said the giant matter-of-factly. 'So now you have a great Hall and people to do whatever you want … and yet you still come looking for a giant.'

'Yes,' said Ethel slowly. 'But I'm not lonely. I can't be lonely. I've got M'um Margot — she's sort of the steward, in charge of everything at the Hall. And the Grand Marshal, he's building walls to keep out the T'manians if they ever decide to come up north again, and all the servants — Everything I do has to be what the Lady does,' she went on in a rush. 'I wanted to do something for myself.'

'So you came giant hunting,' said the giant.

'I suppose,' said Ethel.

The giant looked at her consideringly. 'As it happens,' she said. 'I'm lonely too. Come on then. What's your name?

'Ethel.'

'Come then, Ethel. Let's see how you like a giant's company for a change.'

Her ankle hurt now the thong had been removed, but not enough to slow her down. Ethel followed the giant through the piles of rubble. The crows had vanished now, as though they recognised who had the rights to the dead animals on the hill.

'Are you … are you really a giant?' Ethel asked.

The giant turned and grinned her toothy grin. 'What kind of a question is that?' she demanded. 'Look at me! What do you see? Am I a giant or not? Or maybe you think I'm an elf in disguise, just pretending to be big.'

'Well, of course you're big,' said Ethel. 'I just thought giants would be different.'

'Giants are giants,' said the giant. 'We're big, that's all. If you're big you're a giant.'

'Oh,' said Ethel. 'You mean there are more of you? More giants? But I thought giants didn't exist. The old books say giants don't exist.'

'Maybe they didn't then,' said the giant. 'I bet those olden days writers said unicorns didn't exist either. And geep. But they do now.'

'Why?' asked Ethel.

The giant shrugged. 'All I know is that once there were many horses and now there are hardly any horses and every so often one is born as a unicorn. And once there were many people but now there are fewer, and every so often one is born who becomes a giant ... or something else.'

'Weren't you always a giant?'

The giant shook her head above the heaps of rubble. 'Once I was a baby just as you were a baby. I was a child just like you are a child. But I grew. I kept on growing. I grew till my father could no longer pretend I might change back to true proportions. I became a giant.'

The giant trudged between the final circle of rubble, out into the clearing. 'Come,' she said. 'The door is on the other side.'

Ethel gazed around. The world below was flat, and marked like a game of noughts and crosses. There was the village, with its paddocks of corn and pumpkins and seedy wattles and potatoes. There was a square that must be the Hall, a smudge that was the coast, a green haze that was the forest, a sweep of blue that was the sea and a wider arch that was the sky. She hadn't noticed how high the giant's hill was before. 'You can see everything from here!' she breathed.

The giant smiled a little sadly. 'See everything and be part of nothing,' she answered. 'I can see the boats on the sea and the travellers on the road and the children playing hay fights after harvest.'

'How come you didn't see me coming then?' asked Ethel.

'Because I was inside,' said the giant simply. 'Most days I'm outdoors in the garden. Nothing much escapes me then. Though I don't know whether it makes you more or less lonely to watch others. But if the T'manians ever come to this part of the world I'll be the first to see them; and if a battle's fought I'll watch it too; and weddings and processions and funerals and harvests …' The giant's voice trailed away.

'You said …' began Ethel hesitantly. 'You said there were more giants. Why don't you live with them?'

'And make a land of giants?' The giant laughed a little shrilly. 'There aren't enough of us for that, child. If we were together where folk could see us they'd be scared, and scared people do all sorts of things they wouldn't otherwise. No, we're safest by ourselves, most of the time at any rate; monsters that people can forget, unless they want a reason to be scared. This way, child. This way.'

Ethel followed the giant through the garden. It was

very like the enclosed garden at the Hall, she thought, sheltered from frost and harsh salt winds, though the Hall's garden was surrounded by a neat stone wall and this wall was … she grinned to herself. She had been going to say like a giant had just dropped great chunks of rubble round the edges, which was probably exactly what had happened.

But these gardens flourished, even more than the Hall's. There were beds of white flowered beans, tall as her knees, and beds of parsley, kumera, medi-grass, thyme and sage, and rows of purple cabbages, and green ones, fat as Sam the Miller's belly, and a high stone bed with tomatoes, red and yellow and green striped, trailing over its edges, and tall plants with slightly furry leaves that looked like weeds to Ethel but were too carefully placed to be weeds. Perhaps the giant liked to eat weeds, she thought; or maybe the plants were just hardier up here on the hill than many of those that grew at Uncle's or the Hall.

'You were lucky,' said the giant conversationally. 'Usually anything that comes this way is caught in my traps long before they reach as high as you did. Maybe I need to set more snares.'

'Do you catch a lot of people?' asked Ethel, skirting a bed of strawberries, fruit dark red against the darker leaves.

'For mercy's sake, no,' said the giant. 'It's been … how long has it been? Three years at least since I last caught a person, and that was just a geepherder who had wandered up this way. I caught his geep too, but that I kept. Fear is the best barrier, better than any moat or wall. The snares are mostly to catch animals, wallabies and rabbits and geep, and sometimes even a cow … ah yes, I do like the taste of cow. Meat to eat and meat to keep on a cow, if it's not too old and bony.'

'I saw cow bones,' offered Ethel.

The giant nodded. 'I throw the big ones down,' she said. 'They smell a bit, but they help keep people off. There's nothing as frightening as a good sun-bleached skull. Speaking of smells …'

They rounded the corner of the hut. The giant nodded towards a barrel. 'I'm sorry about the stench. I keep my pottings and the leavings of the animals and soak them well, then pour them down the hill. It makes the grass grow green, and green grass lures the animals. More than I need mostly. Are you hungry?'

Ethel nodded.

'It won't be what you're used to at the Hall,' the giant warned.

'I don't mind. Um … excuse me please for asking …'

'Yes? What is it child?'

'What's your name?' asked Ethel.

The giant paused. 'Do you know how long it is since I had a name?' she asked. 'I'm the giant on the hill ...' She looked down at the world below for a moment, then back at Ethel. 'My name is Alice,' she said finally. 'Alice of ... Alice of the Hill.'

'Thank you, M'um Alice,' said Ethel. She hesitated. 'My name is Ethel.'

The giant blinked at the word 'M'um'. And then she smiled.

The interior of the hut was larger than Ethel had thought it would be from the outside. M'um Alice must have had some skill in piling chunks of rubble together, she thought. The walls sloped gradually up to the tree trunk ceiling, the crevices packed with mud and hay to stop the draughts. A blackened smoke hole at one end covered a broad flat hearth, with a spit for roasting meat and a thick pot of precious iron swung on a hob.

A line of smoked meat hung from the tree trunk beam above the fireplace: legs of geep and wallaby, shoulder of cow, even whole rabbits with their paws hanging down like they were preparing to dive into the fire, all greyed and hard fleshed from long smoking, and glistening slightly from old fat. The hut smelt of old fires and charred bone and bunches of bay leaves, mint bush, tea tree and lavender — not an unpleasant smell, thought Ethel.

The floor was dirt, but so hard trodden it seemed like stone. A broom of tea tree branches leant against the wall.

There was little furniture in the room — a flat-topped chunk of debris that served as a table, a pile of untrimmed furs that must be M'um Alice's bed; a wooden chest, once finely carved but now charred at one edge, to keep cloth from the damp and moths perhaps, if indeed M'um Alice had any clothes other than what she wore. Another flat-topped rock that must be her scriptorium, with leather flask for ink and magpie feather pen and a large flat book still open.

A book ... Ethel stared in the dim light. How would a giant have a book?

M'um Alice followed her gaze. 'Haven't you ever seen a book before?' she asked gently.

'Yes ... of course ... there's a whole room of old books at the Hall. Wonderful books. I bought a new book for the Hall just last month, too. I have the money now to buy books.' She approached the book slowly.

'Can you read?' asked M'um Alice suddenly.

'Yes,' said Ethel, her eyes still on the book.

'How did you learn?'

Ethel looked up guiltily, till she remembered that there was no reason to feel guilty now. She was the

Lady of the Unicorn. She could do anything she wanted, even read.

'A storyteller came to Uncle's village. He had three books — not genuine old ones, but rewritten with pen and ink, not magic-print from olden days. And he had another book too, one that he'd written himself, stories that were all his own.'

'And he taught you to read?'

Ethel shook her head. 'He taught Katerina the Pig Keeper's daughter. They were wealthy from the pigs and could afford to keep the storyteller for a half year. Katerina taught me. She was a good friend, the only person who ever liked me when I was just Ethel.'

'Where is she now?' asked M'um Alice gently, as though she guessed.

'She died of the flushed cough the winter before the unicorn chose me. She would still be my friend now that I'm the Lady, if she'd lived. But it was her who taught me to read.' Ethel looked up a little shyly. 'You're the first person I've met since I became Lady who likes me just because I'm me. You have nothing to gain from my being the Lady.'

'But you must have other friends now?' asked M'um Alice.

Ethel shook her head. 'Someone who wants something from you can't be your friend,' she said.

'You may be right,' said M'um Alice. 'Friends give both ways. The M'um Margot that you spoke of …'

Ethel shrugged. 'She likes the Lady, not me. If I wasn't the Lady she'd pay no attention to me. And she's always telling me what to do, what the last Lady did.'

'And you resent it?'

'I am the Lady!' cried Ethel. 'They are my lands, my Hall, my people. The unicorn chose *me* — but it's always M'um Margot who decides what I should do.'

'And you think a girl of your age should decide what to do?'

'Of course. I'm the Lady of the Unicorn.'

The giant shook her head and stepped carefully to the other end of the hut. Her head nearly touched the ceiling, Ethel realised. A room that was tall for her was cramped for a giant. The giant reached over to the hob.

'Listen to me, girl. Maybe the day will come when your people will follow you. Maybe it won't. But it will depend on you, not on whether a unicorn chose you or not.'

'I don't understand. How would you know about these things?'

'How would a giant on a hilltop know about people? I was a person too once.' The giant nodded towards the book. 'And I read. Books are the essence of people. I know more people on my hilltop than you do in your Hall.'

'Where ... where do you get the books?' asked Ethel tentatively.

'How do you think?' asked M'um Alice with a touch of aggression. 'I steal them. I sneak down from my hill at night, down to Halls and churches, and I rip the doors off their hinges and grab the books, the old-steel goblets, the precious plastic relics, the hangings from the walls ...'

'Don't be silly,' said Ethel.

M'um Alice grinned. 'As to that,' she said. 'I don't know where they come from.'

'You mean a dragon just drops them from the sky?' demanded Ethel scornfully.

'Some were always here. Some a friend brings. He knows I like books. He's better than I am at scavenging from farms and villages. I'm too big. No one could fail to notice me. But I don't know where the books come from.'

'Maybe he steals them,' Ethel pointed out. 'Why don't you ask him?'

The giant laughed. 'It would do no good. He does what he wants. Maybe one day you'll meet him. Then you'll understand.'

'I would be honoured to meet a friend of yours, M'um Alice,' said Ethel politely, though in truth she wasn't sure.

'Maybe. Maybe,' said M'um Alice. She pulled the pot from the hob, then two plates from beside the hearth. They were ordinary earthenware plates, roughly glazed, the sort you'd find in any cottage, thought Ethel, with high rimmed sides to stop the gravy spilling. M'um Alice poured a mess into both of them and handed one to Ethel.

'Thank you,' said Ethel.

'No spoons,' said M'um Alice. 'My friend hasn't brought me spoons, though he brought me a knife once. Maybe he doesn't know what spoons are for. I use a stick to stir my pots. It serves well enough.' She shrugged. 'If my fingers were nimbler I could carve a spoon. But my hands are better at tossing boulders than carving.'

Ethel scooped up a little of her stew in her fingers. The meat was unfamiliar and strongly flavoured. Wallaby perhaps, thought Ethel, certainly not cow or geep, flavoured with onions and some kind of herb, and thick with beans and wattleseed and carrots.

M'um Alice ate hungrily, the gravy dripping down her arm. She licked it clean, then saw Ethel watching. She shrugged. 'It's been a long time since I shared a meal with a person,' she apologised.

'What about your friend?'

'He's different,' said M'um Alice.

'You mean he's not a person?'

M'um Alice wiped her plate clean with her fingers, then hesitated. 'Am I a person?' she asked.

'Of course,' said Ethel.

'Even though I'm a giant?'

'Yes. You are a giant and a person.'

'Well,' said M'um Alice. 'My friend is a person and he is not a person too.'

'Tell me more!' insisted Ethel.

M'um Alice shook her head. 'You would have to meet him to understand,' she said.

'Then let me meet him!'

'You'd be scared.'

'I'm not scared of anything.'

'Not of the T'manians?'

Ethel thrust out her chin. 'Certainly not of the T'manians,' she declared. 'The first thing I did when I became Lady was to prepare the Hall in case of an invasion.'

'How did you do that?' inquired M'um Alice.

'I hired Grand Marshal Kevin and his guard. He's in charge of the new defences. A new wall and … and … all sorts of strategies. He's fought the T'manians many, many times. He told us so. He was even the Marsh King's Grand Marshal for a while.'

'What's he doing this far north then?' inquired

M'um Alice. 'There's never been a T'manian invasion near here.'

'He said he needed a new challenge,' Ethel said vaguely. 'Like our Hall. Our Hall was never built to be defended.'

'There's never been anything to defend it against,' said M'um Alice.

Ethel shrugged. 'The City Lord was telling me last trading day that the T'manians are moving northwards, and that they no longer just raid and kill and leave. There are rumours that their islands are overcrowded, that they want new lands now, and slaves to work them. So they are sailing their boats to lands that aren't prepared for them, so they can take them for themselves. But if the T'manians come here we'll fight them, and we'll win.'

'Will you now?' said M'um Alice softly. She paused. 'Well, what of the night then? Are you afraid of the night? My friend only comes here in the night.'

'The night,' Ethel hesitated. Night was shadow time, whisper time ... 'Why at night?'

'So no one sees him.'

'I'm not scared of the night either,' said Ethel firmly.

'Tonight then,' said the giant calmly. Too calmly, thought Ethel, suddenly aware she may have been manipulated. Had M'um Alice planned for her to meet this friend all along? Would they ...

'Don't worry,' said M'um Alice. She grinned again, showing her too long teeth, a piece of meat caught between them. 'He won't hurt you, I give you my word. He'll be glad I have another friend. Perhaps you will be his friend, too.'

Ethel nodded.

The Hall smelt staler than usual, even though the windows were wide open, and the shutters, too, and there was fresh smelling mint bush in the holders along the walls. M'um Margot looked after the Hall well, thought Ethel.

It was an old Hall, almost as old as the olden days, built like most Halls of the rubble from an olden days building, so it resisted all weathers, not slowly crumbling like the mud and wattle cottages. The walls were thick and the top windows even still had glass — not olden days glass, it was true, but the thick bluish glass from the next-to-olden days, when such crafts as glassmaking were still practised.

The main room was the hall, after which the building took its name, a long room that took almost two minutes to walk, it was so long. According to legend it had been the trading Hall, the meeting Hall in the next-to-olden days, and the other rooms had grown around it to accommodate the Lady.

Behind the Hall itself were the storerooms, full of tallies from farm and village. No cottage stores were as secure from rats or weather as the Hall's. Produce was stored at the Hall and strictly tallied, so each knew what they had brought and could take back again. And by tradition the Lady and her household took what they needed.

The Hall looked after the granary as well, the mill where oats and wattleseed and bunya nuts were dried into flours. According to tradition the Lady controlled all that she could see but, by tradition too, she did very little ruling. She was here to make decisions if decisions were needed — but they rarely were.

Ethel looked out over the courtyard, at the rust-coloured chickens clucking through the unicorn droppings, at the sparrows eyeing them thoughtfully from the eaves, as though they would like to join in but didn't dare, at the unicorn itself, only his nose visible through his stable, and the flash of his silver horn.

'My Lady.'

Ethel turned. It was M'um Margot.

M'um Margot was no taller than Ethel and not much wider. Her hair was hidden under a shallow headdress in plain colours, blue sometimes or red. She wore the traditional narrow skirts of the Hall, unlike the wide dress of the cottager who needed to be able to move freely round their fields or gather oranges perhaps in the generous fabric of their skirts. Ethel was thankful that as the Lady her skirts were wide as well — the Lady's skirts had to be wide or else she wouldn't have been able to ride the unicorn.

'The pumpkin harvest tallies are ready for you to inspect, my Lady,' said M'um Margot, her face expressionless as always below her headdress. She coughed gently. 'They were ready this morning, but you weren't to be found.'

'No,' said Ethel. 'I was out.'

'So it would appear,' said M'um Margot, her voice as blank as her face. 'Of course the Lady of the Unicorn may come and go as she pleases.' She paused slightly for emphasis. 'But the farmers always bring their pumpkin harvest tallies to the Lady on this day. They expected to see you.'

'Well, I didn't know,' said Ethel impatiently. 'No one told me I was expected to be here today.'

'No one expected you to leave the Hall without announcing it, my Lady,' said M'um Margot, fitting her fingers together calmly. They were wide, practical fingers, calloused slightly, but without the ingrained dirt and scars of outdoor workers.

Ethel shrugged. 'I'll count the tallies now,' she said. 'I'm sure they're correct anyway.'

'As you will, my Lady,' said M'um Margot. 'Then tonight there'll be the formal acceptance of the pumpkins. The farmers will arrive at dusk and then you'll ...'

'Yes, yes,' said Ethel. 'Whatever you like. No,' she said suddenly. 'I can't tonight.'

'You can't, my Lady?'

'I ... I have to go out.'

'But ...' M'um Margot closed her lips. It is not my business to question the Lady, her face seemed to say. Even if the Lady is unreasonable.

'Look,' sighed Ethel. 'I'm sorry. I mean it. If I'd known today was special ... Can the farmers come tomorrow night? The pumpkins will still be all right tomorrow. I'll be here then, I promise.'

'There's no reason why they can't come tomorrow,' admitted M'um Margot finally. 'It isn't how it was done before. But I can send a message to them all.'

'Thank you,' said Ethel.

'As my Lady pleases,' said M'um Margot.

Dinner was formal. Dinner was always formal, thought Ethel from her position at the head table in the Hall, M'um Margot on one side and Grand Marshal Kevin on the other.

There was always a cloth on the head table and flowers,

a fancy of M'um Margot's, even though you couldn't eat them. The chairs were always in the same positions, everyone sat in the same places and the meal never started until the Lady took her first mouthful. Ethel had never dared be late in case everyone else went hungry.

The fire licked and puffed and snickered behind the main table, filling the Hall with extra heat, even though it was already hot with the warmth of so many bodies.

Of course it made sense to have a formal meal with so many to be fed. It just looked so … so complicated, thought Ethel wearily. The guards, the millers, the tanner, the chookman, the servants down the far end of the Hall, the platters in place along the tables, roast geep and mounds of small white geep cheese wrapped in herbs, yesterday's leftovers turned into pies, dishes of potatoes, their skins just lifting, spread with butter and still steaming, pumpkins baked whole and filled with long cooked wattleseed and fruit, apple fritters that would be cold before anyone got to eat them, lillypillies baked in honey and bunya bread and wilted turnip tops with bacon and …

Meal times had seemed so luxurious to the village girl, used to the grudging soup at Uncle Maddox's. But to the Lady of the Unicorn it was yet another day's chore to get through, a time when she must be public and watched by all.

'A fine meal,' said Grand Marshal Kevin, his face as smooth as an egg and slightly greasy round the chin. 'But then every meal is fine in your Hall, my Lady. The hospitality of your Hall compares even to the great Halls and I've seen many of them in my day. Why I remember when I was Grand Marshal to the Marsh King, his Hall once served ...'

'Excuse me,' said M'um Margot. 'My Lady, will you have some cheese?'

'Thank you,' said Ethel. 'What were you saying Grand Marshal?'

Grand Marshal Kevin was tall, though not quite as tall as all heroes ought to be, and dark haired. His hands were smooth as his sword, a genuine olden days one he claimed, though M'um Margot sniffed when he was out of hearing and muttered that there were precious few references to swords in any of the olden books.

'I was speaking of the Marsh King,' continued the Grand Marshal affably. 'It was the victory feast after we'd routed the T'manians that third time. Three hundred of them attacked that time ...'

'Are you sure, Grand Marshal?' asked M'um Margot politely. 'You would need many boats to carry three hundred. Of course I've never seen a T'manian boat, but I have heard they only carry a crew of ten or even less. Now that would mean that to carry three hundred there would have to be …'

M'um Margot didn't like Grand Marshal Kevin. M'um Margot didn't like anyone new, thought Ethel resentfully. Including her.

'What do the T'manian boats look like, Grand Marshal?' put in Ethel hurriedly, though in fact she was glad she'd been too young to remember anything about the T'manian attack that had killed her parents. 'Are they really made of metal? Surely they'd sink?'

For once the Grand Marshal looked serious. 'Yes, my Lady. They're made of metal. Some people believe that the T'manians have great stores of metal, olden days cities perhaps that weren't covered by the floods. But I don't believe that is the case. Metal is the first thing they steal on their raids; metal and slaves and just enough food to see them home to their islands.

'But this is a poor subject for a lady's table, my Lady! And there's no need for you to worry about the T'manians now. Not when you'll soon have fine walls …'

'When will the walls be started?' put in M'um Margot.

'Soon, soon,' said the Grand Marshal good-temperedly. 'You can't hurry these things. As soon as we have the stone …'

Ethel swallowed another mouthful of cheese. What was M'um Alice eating? she wondered, high up on her hill. Perhaps she should bring her some chicken tonight. Did M'um Alice ever catch chicken in her traps? The roast at the end of the high table was still untouched. Suddenly she realised the Grand Marshal was still speaking. 'I'm sorry Grand Marshal Kevin,' she said. 'What was that again?'

'I was saying, my Lady,' said the Grand Marshal jovially, 'that when I was in the service of Lord Jason ...'

'I thought you were in the service of the King,' said M'um Margot.

'I served the Lord Jason before I was in the service of the King.' Grand Marshal Kevin was unfazed. 'Lord Jason was Overlord of the estuary up beyond the great salt marshes. But as I was saying ...'

What would it be like to live by yourself like M'um Alice? wondered Ethel. To snare your own food and grow your own crops, to watch the sunset spread across the world all by yourself. Lonely, perhaps; but you could be lonely in a crowded hall as well ...

'My Lady? My Lady?'

Ethel blinked, brought back abruptly to the present. 'I'm sorry?' she asked. 'I didn't catch what you said.'

'It doesn't matter, my Lady,' said M'um Margot.

Ethel glanced at the waterclock in the courtyard. You could just see its steady drip, drip, drip through the open doors. 'Grand Marshal Kevin, M'um Margot, if you will excuse me. I have an appointment.'

'An appointment?' Grand Marshal Kevin raised his eyebrows. 'Ah, a young man. What other appointment could a lady as beautiful as yourself …'

'The Lady is too young for young men,' said M'um Margot shortly.

'When a lady is as charming as our Lady,' began Grand Marshal Kevin. He took another mouthful of stuffed tomato. 'I remember when …'

Ethel slipped from the table.

The unicorn sniffed his way between the rubble, his hooves sounding hollow on the soft grass. He seemed to see better in the darkness than a horse would, thought Ethel. Which was strange, as you'd think that a creature so bright and white would only love the day.

The moon sailed like a cheese rind above the hill, thickening the shadows between the rocks. The smell wasn't as bad as it had been during the day, Ethel decided.

She shuddered as the unicorn stepped over a giant skull, milk white in the moonlight, then sat herself firmly upright. It was just a bullock's skull. She ate beef on festival days. Why should she be scared of its skull? Why should darkness make everything so strange?

How could anyone live mostly in darkness, like M'um Alice's friend? she wondered. How would it change you to know only shadows and never the clear light of day?

The rubble grew thicker. Ethel dismounted and led the unicorn up the final path. She halted at the edge of the clearing and looked for a stout beam or post to tie him to. Yes, there was a bean pole. She looped the reins over the top and knotted them firmly.

Suddenly the unicorn reared, his pale hooves flashing in the night. The bean pole cracked, torn from the garden and swung in a wild arc against his back.

'What's wrong?' cried Ethel.

The unicorn reared again, snorting his fright.

'What is it? Quiet boy … quiet …'

'You'd better take him down the hill again.' It was M'um Alice's voice. Ethel turned. The giant seemed even taller in the moonlight, her bulk blocking out a good portion of the stars.

'But what's wrong with him?'

'He smells someone strange,' said M'um Alice. 'It upsets him. You'd better tether him further down. There's a post over that way. There's a snare on it, but it's not set. You'll see it in a minute.'

'But ...' Ethel had been going to say that M'um Alice was strange and the unicorn hadn't been afraid of her. But she didn't. She patted the unicorn's neck instead to soothe him and led him across the hill and down.

The unicorn was breathing heavily but not from exertion. His sides were sweaty.

'I should rub you down,' said Ethel. 'But there's no breeze here. You won't get chilled will you?'

The unicorn snorted, but not as loudly this time. His eyes flashed white, and then he sighed and bent down to the grass and began to eat.

Ethel turned up towards the clearing again.

M'um Alice was waiting for her. 'Scared?' she asked abruptly.

Ethel shook her head.

'Maybe you should be,' suggested M'um Alice. 'Your horse is scared.'

'He's a unicorn,' stated Ethel.

'Ah yes, of course he is, how could I have missed it?' said M'um Alice.

'He really is,' said Ethel. 'It's not just the horn. If you put him with other horses they attack him. They know he's different.'

M'um Alice nodded again, her face serious now. 'They always attack what's different,' she said. 'Humans or horses …' She paused in front of the door. 'Child,' she said hesitantly.

'I'm not a child,' said Ethel. 'I'm the Lady of the Unicorn. Whatever is in there won't hurt me.'

'Won't hurt you perhaps,' said M'um Alice softly. 'But you might hurt him.'

'Me? How?'

'By showing revulsion. By turning away.' M'um Alice hesitated again. 'Perhaps I shouldn't have asked you here tonight,' she said. 'I don't know why I did — loneliness perhaps. He's a good friend, the one who's here tonight, but not someone to talk to as you talked to me.'

'I won't hurt him,' said Ethel softly. 'I promise M'um Alice.'

M'um Alice looked at her closely. 'I believe you,' she said finally. 'Very well, child. Come in.'

The inside of the hut was dim, lit by a single taper on the table. The fire licked red tongues up the rough chimney, the stones behind it black. M'um Alice took the taper and lit a slush lamp and then another. The room flickered in the growing light.

Ethel looked round. 'But where …' she began. And then she stopped.

A creature sat by the hearth, its back to the flames. It was small, which was why she hadn't seen it at first. It had four legs, furry legs like a dog, or cat perhaps, thought Ethel. Its face was furry too, and its ears and snout were long and covered in hair as well. Its teeth were very white and protruded a little at the edges of its mouth, like a wolf.

But this was human.

How she knew she couldn't tell. It was like no human she had ever seen. But somehow Ethel knew that despite the fur and teeth and hairy ears, this was no animal.

The creature saw her. It started in sudden alarm, as though its sight and hearing were too poor to have seen or heard her when she first came in. He backed away towards the fire. The heat stopped him. He crouched trembling in the firelight.

'Sit down,' said M'um Alice to Ethel gently. 'Try not to startle him.'

Ethel sat. The weathered concrete chair was too tall for her to reach comfortably, but she clambered up anyway and sat on its edge, her legs dangling and her back very straight.

'Tell him I won't hurt him,' she said softly.

'Tell him yourself,' said M'um Alice. 'He doesn't understand words. Just voices and how you say things. Say you're his friend and he might understand.'

Like the unicorn, thought Ethel. 'Hello,' said Ethel tentatively. The creature looked up at her with large brown eyes. 'My name's Ethel,' she added softly. 'What's yours?'

'I call him Hingram,' said M'um Alice. 'It's not his name, of course. I had a brother once …' She shook her head. 'Hingram, this is a friend,' she said quietly. 'Would you like another friend?'

Hingram blinked at her inquiringly, then looked back at Ethel.

'Try feeding him something,' suggested M'um Alice. She walked over to the store cupboard by the door and pulled out a shank of geep, greasy with cold fat. 'Try this.'

Ethel wriggled off the chair and took the meat. She crossed the room warily and held it out towards the boy. 'Here,' she said slowly. 'Are you hungry?'

Suddenly the boy snatched the meat. He held it close to his chest and warily retreated again. He sniffed it, and then began to gnaw.

Ethel went back to her seat and clambered up. 'How can he be a friend? You can't talk to him, or …'

'Friends help each other,' said M'um Alice. 'That's how we met. I'd been trapping down below and Hingram, well I reckon he came after the scent of meat. He can't catch much for himself so he scavenges.'

'You mean … stuff that's already dead?' Ethel suppressed a shudder.

M'um Alice shrugged. 'He forages what he can. I had known someone was around. I'd seen him out of the corner of my eye. Never fully, you understand, Hingram was too wary for that. So I left bits of meat out for him, and vegetables too, though he never ate those, and sometimes fruit. He liked fruit, too …

'But that day something else came after the scent of meat. A lion. I should have seen it coming, but lions are the colour of the rocks. I've never seen a lion around here before or since, though I've seen prides in the distance, way off on the plains beyond the forest. They hunt in packs, you know. Maybe this one had been cast out of its pack. Animals can do strange things when they're cast out.'

Ethel shook her head. 'I've never seen one.'

'Let's hope you don't,' said M'um Alice. Her thick fingers brushed a strand of hair from her face. 'It must have been hungry because it leapt on me, big as I am. And big as I am it had me down and I was fighting it off my throat. I still have the scars.' She held up one broad arm.

'And then it dropped away, right off me. It just lay there …'

'Dead?' asked Ethel.

'Not dead. Stunned. It lay there for a while then blinked and slunk away and it's never come back either. Frighten something enough and it doesn't return.

'But it was Hingram who had saved me. He'd grabbed a rock and leapt up onto the boulder — that big one straight out there and threw it down onto the beast's head.

'He didn't have to save me. He could have let the lion take me, then taken my hut for his own, and scavenged from my traps and had all the meat he wanted …

'But he was my friend. And he's been my friend ever since.'

The fire crackled and flared. Hingram started back and then relaxed. He sucked at the marrow from the shank, then threw the bone into the fire. The scent of charred bone filled the hut. He looked around hungrily.

'May I give him some more?' asked Ethel.

M'um Alice nodded.

'Oh,' said Ethel. 'I just remembered. I brought you some chicken. From the kitchens at the Hall. It's in the saddlebag on the unicorn.'

Ma'm Alice smiled. 'That was kind of you,' she said. 'It'll be good to taste something I haven't caught myself and cooked myself. And chicken … well, I don't get chicken in my traps. But …' She stopped as Hingram scurried across the floor.

He walked on four legs, not two, thought Ethel. She froze as Hingram stopped by her chair. He raised his head and quickly licked her leg, then backed away, as though he was ready for a blow. Another pause and he was gone, a shadow through the door.

'I thought he would leave soon,' said M'um Alice. 'He never stays long.'

'Who is he?' asked Ethel. 'Where does he come from?'

M'um Alice shook her head. 'I don't know,' she answered. 'He can't speak … I don't think he hears well enough to learn to speak, and his eyesight is none too good as well. But his sense of smell seems to make up for it.

'No, I don't know where he came from. If he had parents who cast him out, or who died and left him alone. If he was born like that or just grew … differently. I don't know.' She crossed over to the fire and threw more wood on — a giant root, a tree root perhaps, thought Ethel. Only someone as big as M'um Alice could have managed it.

'Why did you want me to meet him?' she asked finally.

M'um Alice sat heavily on the other slab chair. 'I don't know,' she said quietly. 'Perhaps … perhaps I thought that the Lady of the Unicorn should know someone different, to learn a little understanding perhaps. Or maybe I just wanted one friend to meet another.'

An owl boomed outside. 'Am I your friend?' asked Ethel finally. 'I would like to have a friend.'

'Doesn't the Lady of the Unicorn have friends?' asked M'um Alice.

'No,' said Ethel. 'Loyal subjects. But I left my friends behind when I became the Lady. When I was ... different.'

'Friends then,' said M'um Alice. She licked her wide dark lips. 'Now, where is that chicken you said that you brought?'

The moon was low on the horizon, as though someone swung it from a string high up in the night sky. Ethel untethered her unicorn. He whinnied at her softly and pressed his nose against her, as though checking that she smelt the same despite the unfamiliar scents that clung to her.

Ethel glanced down the hill. She could just see the Hall from here, a dim light in the dark. 'It's later than I thought,' she said. 'M'um Margot will be worried.'

'Won't she be asleep?' asked M'um Alice. The roast chicken looked tiny in her hand, like a roast sparrow, not a hen, thought Ethel.

'No. She never sleeps before I do, I think.'

'A loyal woman,' said M'um Alice.

Ethel sighed. 'Loyal to the Lady,' she said. 'To the idea of the Lady. Not to me. I don't think she even likes me. She loved the last Lady very much.' She gathered the unicorn's tether in her hand. 'I'll mount when we get down the hill,' she said. 'It will be lighter there, away from the rubble. Thank you for your hospitality, M'um Alice. And for introducing me to your friend.'

'It's good to have friends,' said M'um Alice vaguely. She met Ethel's eyes for a moment. 'I do have other friends,' she said slowly. 'Not ones I see often, but friends none the less. Maybe one day you would like to meet them too?'

'Friends like Hingram?'

'No. Not like Hingram. There's no one else like Hingram. But not like the people of the village or the farms or the Hall either. These are forest people.'

'I didn't know there were forest people,' said Ethel. 'Grand Marshal Kevin says there are dragons in the forest.'

'No dragons,' said M'um Alice. 'A few kangaroos. Possums. A colony of bats. And people. Different people.'

'People like you?'

'Some like me. A bit. Some different in other ways.'

'I would like to meet them,' said Ethel slowly.

'Are you sure?'

'Yes,' said Ethel.

M'um Alice nodded. 'Next full moon then. That's when we meet — at the full moon.'

For a moment Ethel hesitated. Witches met at full moon, and werewolves bared their teeth … it didn't take much of a leap of imagination to see Hingram as a werewolf.

Then she shook herself. She was being silly. Hingram was no werewolf. He was a boy, a different boy. And it made sense for the outcasts of the forest to meet at full moon when there was more light to see by.

'Will I meet you here?' she asked.

M'um Alice nodded. 'At dusk,' she said. 'When everyone is indoors. There's just time for me to walk to the forest and meet my friends then come back here before the world is awake and people see me.' She grinned in the darkness. 'I travel fast,' she said. 'I have long legs. But perhaps your unicorn can keep up with me.'

'Of course he can,' declared Ethel proudly.

'We'll see,' said M'um Alice.

'I hate darning,' said Ethel.

'But it must be done, my Lady,' said M'um Margot.

'Not by me,' said Ethel.

'But the Lady always mends the tapestries, my Lady.'

'I am the Lady,' said Ethel. 'And this Lady doesn't darn. Anyway, I'd make a mess of it.' She glanced out the window. The sky arched like a blue glazed bowl held upside down, the breeze smelt of forest and far hills. She wanted to be outside, not stifling by the fire. 'I'm going to inspect the defence wall,' she said. 'Grand Marshal Kevin said they would start to dig the foundations today.'

M'um Margot looked back down at her darning. 'I believe he has had to postpone it again, my Lady,' she said. 'He said something about needing more materials. He has gone to Far-marsh Castle with his men.'

'But he'd just got back from getting new materials,' said Ethel. 'He said he needed to arrange a supply of dressed stone.'

'And now perhaps he needs stonemasons, my Lady,' said M'um Margot.

'But …' Ethel hesitated. M'um Margot was antagonistic enough about the Marshal. There was no point making it worse. And after all, there was no real hurry for the walls.

'He knows what he's doing,' Ethel said finally. 'After all, he was the King's defender. He's built defence walls all along the coast. He told me about the walls he built at the salt marshes just last night.'

'Yes, my Lady,' said M'um Margot, attending once more to her darning.

Ethel wondered if she'd even listened.

The moon rose fat and yellow, like it was a duckling stuffed full of grass ready to make its first swim across the sky. Ethel ignored the stares of the Hall workers as she crossed the hard packed rubble courtyard. The unicorn lifted his head as she approached, his mouth full of thistle from the crevices between the stones, his coat gleaming white against the mud and rubble walls.

Ethel rode slowly between the gates then turned the unicorn point forward to the hill. Let them stare, she thought. She was the Lady. No one had any right to question where she went, or why.

Especially not M'um Margot.

A child waved to her as she rose between the cottages, then giggled as she waved back. A girl gathering washing from the line gazed at her, curious, the men and women with their hoes nodded respectfully.

I am the Lady, thought Ethel.

The dusk settled as she approached the hill, pink clouds shading into grey. M'um Alice waited among the boulders, her head with its thick ring of plaits towering above them. 'I saw you set out,' she explained.

'You see everything,' said Ethel.

M'um Alice laughed, a booming sound that sent the unicorn skittering. 'Not quite,' she said. 'Not what goes on behind the windows or in the sheds. But I see enough. Come,' she said. 'We have to hurry.'

It was strange travelling through the night, thought Ethel, watching the trees' thin fingers brush against the moon and send the shadows dancing across the road, glancing unseen into the dim interiors of cottages, watching people sitting by the fire or carving, mending or knitting by the light of a single slush lamp on the table.

It was even stranger to be with M'um Alice. What did M'um Alice think when she looked through cottage windows, watching the peaceful everyday life indoors? As far off to her as if she'd been — the Lady of the Unicorn, thought Ethel.

Not that she wanted to live in one of those houses again, mend sheets by the light of a spluttering lamp — M'um Margot came briefly into her mind. Was she still mending by the light of the Hall candles, waiting for her Lady to return?

M'um Alice turned, a solid lump against the night. 'Not too fast for you am I?' she asked softly.

'No,' said Ethel. The unicorn wasn't even straining. A unicorn is hardier than a horse, thought Ethel proudly — stockier and more enduring, even if it didn't have a horse's speed.

'Not far now,' said M'um Alice.

Ethel nodded. Somehow M'um Alice seemed even odder away from her hill, as though up there her size seemed normal against the massive boulders. Even her walk seemed different — not a normal walk like other people, but a sort of lunging hunch. Perhaps, thought Ethel suddenly, there were other things different about M'um Alice apart from her size.

'Tired?' asked M'um Alice.

'No,' said Ethel. 'I slept this afternoon.'

M'um Alice's grin was white in the moonlight. 'What did your people think of that?'

'It's none of their business what I do. I'm their Lady.'

The grin grew wider. It was a big grin even in the enormous face, a little bigger than a normal grin might be. 'I should think that made what you do even more their business,' said M'um Alice.

'But …' Ethel stopped. She had been going to say the people didn't own her. But maybe they did in a way. '*My* Lady,' said M'um Margot.

She didn't want to be theirs. She wanted … What did she want?

'Nearly there,' said M'um Alice.

The forest was a dark mass against the stars, almost purple after the pale gold of the plain. Only the odd branch broke the smooth dark line, dancing firelit against the moon. It was strange to think the forest had been there even in the olden days, too marshy for the olden-dayers to bother with clearing.

The forest would be full of shadows, thought Ethel.

'M'um Alice?'

'Yes?' The giant grinned again. 'It still seems strange to hear you call me by that name.'

'Do you want me to stop?'

'No,' said M'um Alice. 'What were you wanting to ask?'

'Will Hingram be there'

'Maybe,' said M'um Alice. 'He often is. You can never tell though.'

'Will he mind my being there? Will he remember me? Does he realise I'm the one he met at your place?'

'Oh, he realises that well enough. I think he's intelligent, for all he can't hear much or speak or see. More intelligent than you or me perhaps. How would we survive if we couldn't see or hear, if we had to scurry on all fours from babyhood like Hingram?'

'I don't know,' said Ethel.

M'um Alice shrugged. 'Every time I don't see him for a few days I worry. Maybe he's been caught in a trap, or someone has set the dogs on him.'

'But, but they wouldn't!' cried Ethel.

'Of course they would,' said M'um Alice. 'Think back to your farm life girl. What would your aunt have done if she saw a thing like Hingram out the window one dark night.'

'She'd have …' Ethel didn't finish. 'But she'd have been wrong!' she said finally.

'There are lots of wrongs in this world,' said M'um Alice softly.

Of course, M'um Alice would know, thought Ethel, and was silent.

She could smell the forest before they reached it. Why had she never noticed the forest's smell before? Was it stronger at night? Or did the colours of the day just blind you to the scents of night? A damp smell, a soil smell, a rotting smell — but not like garbage rotted. A scent of a thousand years of leaves soaking into swamp. A mosquito buzzed against her arm. She swatted it absent-mindedly.

'We leave the track here,' said M'um Alice. 'You'd better dismount and lead him now. The branches can be low.'

'But how do we find the way?'

M'um Alice chuckled. It was a louder sound now that she no longer had to fear people hearing her. As though she could be more herself in the forest, thought Ethel. 'I know the way,' she said. 'Thirty, no almost forty years I've come this way. You walk behind me, and keep the unicorn behind you too, or you'll find yourself knee-deep in mud.'

'How did you find the way the first time?'

'I was led here,' said M'um Alice, stumping through the trees. Her head was taller than the lowest branches, so she had to duck or hold them back. 'Just as I'm leading you now.'

'By whom?'

'A friend.'

'Who was the friend?' persisted Ethel.

M'um Alice stopped. 'You really want to know?'

'Yes,' said Ethel.

'His name was Justin. He was a leper.'

A leper. For a moment Ethel started back. Perhaps M'um Alice was infected too. But her skin had seemed clear. Surely if she had been infected it would have shown in forty years.

'No, I'm not a leper,' said M'um Alice, as though she'd read her mind. 'Leprosy isn't particularly infectious. In fact for all I know Justin didn't have leprosy at all. But his skin was different, marked and mottled, and these days that makes you a leper. You can read all about leprosy and skin diseases in the old books, though no one bothers. They had cures even for leprosy in the old days.

'Justin found me after I'd been cast out, after I'd begun to grow and kept on growing, so that they could no longer pretend that I was normal. I had no idea how to survive in those days. I went from village to village, hoping someone would take me in …'

There was no self pity in M'um Alice's voice, thought Ethel wonderingly. Her voice was matter-of-fact.

'But of course they didn't. It was at the last village I tried. A woman gave me scraps and told me to go … but that little kindness made me hope for more. I sat on her doorstep, hoping she'd smile at me again, but she screamed at me instead and the children began to throw stones.

'And then Justin came. In his leper's cloak, with his leper's bell, just as in the old days. The children ran away. I nearly ran as well. But he spoke to me kindly and I realised I wanted kindness more than I feared leprosy. In those days of course I couldn't read. I didn't know how little I had to fear.

'Justin lived on my hill. It was his hill then. They called it Leper's Hill then, just as it's the Giant's Hill now. He took me home. He had a shack — just bits of wood propped over the boulders to make a roof. He didn't have my strength,' said M'um Alice, still matter-of-factly. 'He was too weak to hunt, and the lack of food made him weaker still. But he did have books. He'd been a Manor Lord before the disease struck.'

'A Manor Lord wouldn't have been cast out if he had leprosy!' protested Ethel. 'They'd have kept him isolated, but his people would have looked after him.'

'They did — till the T'manians came. The T'manians burnt his Hall, they enslaved his people — but not Justin. No one wants a leper as a slave. In those days the T'manians plundered, then they left. They didn't try to keep the land as they do now. So when they'd gone Justin foraged in the ruins of his Hall and took his books high up on the hill, where he could see if T'manians came again. But they didn't. He saw me instead, and weak as he was he came to rescue me.'

'Did you live with him?' asked Ethel.

M'um Alice nodded, the movement almost hidden by the night. 'Justin had read about traps in his books, though he didn't have the strength to make them. I did. First of all I dug pit traps; just big pits covered with thin bits of wood and with straw on top, so anything that walks on top falls through. But that way injured the animals … it's a cruel way to kill them, and sometimes there were more than we needed, with broken legs perhaps so we couldn't let them go. So I made snares instead.

'I built the hut too, with Justin reading from his books and telling me to put this here, or that bit there, to fetch a tree trunk to brace the doorframe or how to tan skins to make more snares. Gradually I learnt to read as well. I don't know what I would have done up on my hill without my books. Books don't care what you look like. Books speak to anyone who knows their words.

'When he was stronger from good feeding, Justin led me here, into the forest. He hadn't been for years. He'd been too weak to walk this far. But the people were still here. Not the same people — even every month they differ. Some come every month, some live too far away to come too often; some come once and never come again, so you wonder if something has happened to them. Or if being with others who were different made them too aware that they were different too. Come, we must hurry now.'

'But what happened to Justin?' demanded Ethel.

'He died,' said M'um Alice abruptly.

'Of the leprosy?'

'Of old age. He was very old when he found me. But he taught me many things,' said M'um Alice. 'He taught me that by ourselves neither might have survived. But the two of us did very well. And that's why the people of the forest meet.'

'I don't understand,' said Ethel softly.

'You will,' said M'um Alice. 'Friends help each other,' she added softly.

The moon was above the trees now, its beams piercing between the branches, reflecting from the distant pools, the shadows sharp and flickering on the forest floor. Something shrilled above them, then was silent. A possum, Ethel realised, annoyed with the intruders in its world.

'How far now?' inquired Ethel.

M'um Alice pointed to a slight rise in front of them. 'Just through here,' she said.

Ethel squinted through thicker trees, their branches low to the ground, not high and silver trunked like the swamp gums. Fig trees maybe, or pittosporums. M'um Alice parted the branches and crouched low.

Ethel followed her, leading the unicorn behind her.

It was damp and sour smelling under the trees, with ankle deep water. Maidenhair ferns tickled her ankles. The unicorn snorted, or perhaps it was a sneeze. M'um Alice looked even larger, bent double as she squeezed under the trees.

'Up this way,' she instructed, and parted the branches again.

Light poured through. Moonlight, starlight, and firelight as well, red among the gold. Ethel held the branch up to let the unicorn through, then looked around.

They were on a rise above the swamp, fringed with dark trees all around. No one would see the firelight from here Ethel realised, though it was a small fire, the coals glowing red and smokeless; a pile of dry branches set to one side, and a large pot beside it, steaming in the firelight.

Ethel stared at the fire. It was safe to stare at the fire. It meant she didn't have to look at the faces all around.

Slowly she lifted her eyes, and then she stared.

A face looked at her. But it wasn't a face. It was half a face. The rest was … was what? Burnt away by flame, eaten away by illness, savaged by an animal. All that was left was bone and scar and a gaping hole where once there'd been a mouth. And the mouth was smiling. Or trying to smile. She could see a tongue, some teeth …

This wasn't like M'um Alice. This wasn't like Hingram, so small and so defenceless. This was a … monster, monster, monster shrieked Ethel's mind. But it can't be a monster whispered another part of her. This is M'um Alice's friend …

Her gaze shifted slowly from the ruined face and dropped with relief onto the person beside them. This was an old woman. Her back was bent in a sharp curve, so her face nearly touched her knees, then bent out again as though someone had tried to pull it straight. She was smiling, a strangely sweet smile though her face was lined with pain. That sweet smile gave Ethel the courage to look further.

A man, another giant, but not like M'um Alice. Where M'um Alice was tall and broad this man was simply tall, like he'd softened in the sun and been stretched like sticky toffee. His head was almost hairless, his lips were thick and his nose and chin were much too long. He blinked as though confused by the newcomers.

A boy sat beside him, an ordinary boy, till you saw his face was marked by circles, like raised pimples on his skin. And then a girl with sad brown eyes, and hair — thick hair across her face and even down her neck, her hands and feet were hairy. And another giant and another, even larger than M'um Alice, her face blank as the moon, until she smiled, the wide unthinking smile of a tiny child …

Ethel was going to be sick. She was going to run. As soon as her legs would move she'd run. She'd dive under the branches and mount the unicorn and she'd be gone …

Why was she here? She was the Lady of the Unicorn. She had no place with people such as these. Ugly people, people who had no home, monsters …

Suddenly her mind halted. They'd call M'um Alice a monster. But she wasn't. You might even think she was ugly, till you knew her. The first time she'd seen her she'd been the giant; the second time M'um Alice who was big; and now she was M'um Alice and you hardly noticed her size.

And what would happen if she ran? No one would stop her, not even M'um Alice. But she would have lost a friend.

Slowly she raised her head again. The old woman with the hump still smiled at her. Her voice was soft but harsh, a worn out voice. 'Welcome child.'

And suddenly it didn't seem so strange, it didn't seem so horrible. As though words had made a magic to make it all all right.

'Hello,' said Ethel softly.

'So, you can speak,' said the old woman. 'And you look like anyone might look. Why have you brought her here, Alice? Why, if she's not one of us?'

M'um Alice crossed to the fire and held out her hands as though to warm them, although the night was hardly cool. 'She needs friends,' she said slowly. 'So I brought her to meet mine.'

'To laugh at us?' The harsh voice was firm. 'To run away in horror? Look at her. She's still in shock.'

'But she hasn't run,' said M'um Alice. 'Come closer Ethel. Bring the unicorn.'

Obediently Ethel pulled at the reins. The unicorn moved closer to the firelight.

'Ah,' said the old woman. 'I begin to see. You're the new Lady of the Unicorn. Welcome, my Lady.' The tone was only slightly ironic.

'Welcome, my Lady,' a voice echoed. It was the male giant. But the voice was empty, as though there was no meaning in his words.

'That's Philip,' said the old woman. 'He grew too much and his brains went as he grew. For some reason M'um Alice kept her brains. She's the only one of the big 'uns who has. She uses them too. So girl, you are the Lady of the Unicorn?'

'Yes,' said Ethel, her voice steadier now.

'Do you know who we are?' asked the woman.

Ethel nodded. 'You're the people of the forest.'

'Yes. We're the people no one wants. We're the people who have to hide away because we're different.'

'I know,' said Ethel.

The old woman nodded. 'Good, good,' she said. 'You did well to bring her, Alice. You did very well indeed.'

Ethel froze at the tone of her voice. 'What do you mean?' she demanded.

'Why nothing. Nothing,' said the woman. 'Just that I'm glad that you are here.'

'What do you want of me?' asked Ethel quietly. 'You do want something, don't you? I've learnt how people look at me when they hope that I can give them something.'

The old woman shrugged. The movement looked grotesque in the flickering light, her narrow shoulders protruding far beyond her head. 'Hasn't Alice told you why we come here?'

'No,' said Ethel.

'We come to do what we can for each other,' said the old woman. 'Some,' she gestured with an elbow toward the male giant, 'just bring food, a couple of dead roos perhaps, enough food for some of us for days or weeks if we look after it. We look after those who have been hurt and don't have the wits to tend themselves. Some of us exchange news. But all of us bring what we can.'

'M'um Alice didn't bring anything,' said Ethel slowly.

'She brought you,' the old woman's laugh sounded like bits of rusted metal scraping down a pot. 'You're the Lady. You're the best that anyone has brought.'

Ethel turned to M'um Alice. 'Is that true? That you brought me here to be of use to your friends?'

M'um Alice hesitated. 'In a way,' she said.

Ethel clenched her fists. All at once she was angry, angrier than she had ever been in her life.

'What do you intend to do with me? Ransom me? Make M'um Margot deliver bags of corn or iron pots to the forest? Then you'll deliver me to her?'

'No,' said M'um Alice. Her face was expressionless. 'That wasn't what I intended. But yes, I brought you here so you might help.'

Ethel shuddered. Desolation swept across her sharp and swift. 'That's the only reason you said you were friends with me wasn't it? Because I'm the Lady! Because I might help you! Help your friends!'

'No,' said M'um Alice gently, but Ethel spoke over her.

'I thought you were different! I thought you really liked me! But you're just like everyone else! You just want my help!'

'Would it be so very bad to help us?' said the old woman sharply. 'Friends help each other.'

'I'm not your friend!' cried Ethel. 'You want to use me — not be my friend!' Her voice broke off. *Acceptance*, said the old woman's eyes, the scarred half face, the pock-marked boy. *Can you give us acceptance?*

'I'll do what I can! I don't know how I can help but I can try. If you send me a list of what you need …' choked Ethel. Then she was running, running, under the branches out into the forest.

Dimly she heard the unicorn canter behind her. Someone must have sent him after her, lifted the branches for him. The old woman or M'um Alice …

The unicorn nudged her back. Ethel clasped him for a moment, her face against his neck, the old woman's words thudding in her ears. Friends, friends, friends — friends help each other.

'What if I need help?' cried Ethel to the dark branches. 'Then who will help me?' The unicorn turned curiously at the sound of her voice, his ears laid back in alarm. Ethel shook her head. She didn't need help. The Lady of the Unicorn never needed help. She had everything she needed.

Except friends.

Ethel mounted the unicorn. He lifted his head, as though to sniff the path, then picked his way delicately through the swamp, back into the cleared lands and the Hall.

'And twelve pots of macadamia oil,' said Ethel. She gazed around the storeroom, its thick walls roughly plastered with thick clay to keep it cool, the packed rubble floor, packed smooth with mud and straw, the dim light from door and taper. 'Haven't we done enough yet?'

'There are still three more storerooms to be counted, my Lady,' said M'um Margot calmly. 'The Lady always takes stock of the storerooms once a year, to see what needs to be used before the new tallies. It's tradition.'

Ethel sighed, a deep breath filled with the scents of withered apples and sprouted onions, heavy fruit cakes to store the eggs and fruit and nuts, jars of honey crystallised around the edges. Tradition. Just as the Lady always had to eat at the top table with everyone around, instead of eating as she read in the book room, thought Ethel dismally; just as the Lady had to learn the old tongue in case she met another Lady (who would probably rather talk in everyday speech too) or the Lord of Coasttown, instead of exploring the hills and forest on her unicorn …

What would M'um Margot do, Ethel wondered, if she just flung down the tally book and ran across the room, out the courtyard and rode away, up to the …

Up where? she thought bitterly. To M'um Alice? But M'um Alice was just like everyone else. If M'um Alice had met her before the unicorn, she'd have ignored her too. M'um Alice only wanted help for her friends — her real friends.

For a moment she remembered M'um Alice's face in the firelight that night. The too-wide eyes dark, her mouth a straight line. She looked almost as if someone had struck her and she refused to show the pain.

But why should M'um Alice be hurt? The Lady of the Unicorn would help, if she could, when she could …

A flicker of guilt washed over her. She dismissed it firmly. No, she'd done nothing yet for the people of the forest. She'd asked them to send her a list of what they needed. What else could she do? She didn't even know where they lived — the other side of the forest from the Hall, maybe. Except for M'um Alice and Hingram.

Hingram! He hadn't been at the moonlit meeting. What had M'um Alice said? *Every time he doesn't appear, I worry that someone has hurt him. Or maybe not a person, an animal perhaps — a lion …*

Hingram couldn't write a list of what he needed. Hingram couldn't even talk.

'M'um Margot?'

'Yes, my Lady.'

'Is it possible to send a message to all the villages and farms?'

M'um Margot looked surprised. 'Of course, my Lady. The last Lady did it all the time.'

'Then I want it done now.'

'Of course, my Lady,' said M'um Margot cautiously. 'What about?'

'I want it to say …' Ethel tried to think. 'If anyone sees a … a strange boy, with fur down his back and long teeth and …'

'A monster, my Lady!'

'He's not a monster!' said Ethel fiercely. 'Anyway, if anyone sees someone like that …'

'They're to capture it, my Lady?'

'He's not an it. He's a boy. A different boy. They're to … oh, I don't know — to send a message here, at once. To leave out food so he'll come back again — yes, that's it! They're to leave out food. And not to frighten him in any way.'

M'um Margot looked at her curiously. 'And then what, my Lady?'

'Then I will act as I see fit,' stated Ethel. She didn't

have to explain to M'um Margot. She didn't have to explain to anyone!

'Yes, my Lady,' said M'um Margot. 'I'll attend to it directly. Is it my Lady's pleasure to keep on with the tally now?'

Ethel sighed. No, it wasn't her pleasure. It was her duty.

One of the Grand Marshal's guards entered the storeroom. What was his name again? thought Ethel. Tor, that was it. He coughed tentatively to attract her attention. 'My Lady?'

Ethel blinked. 'Yes? What is it?'

'It's a letter, my Lady.' Tor offered it carefully. Letters were rare.

'From whom?'

'I don't know, my Lady. A messenger handed it in at the gates.'

'What did they look like?' demanded Ethel.

'I didn't see them, my Lady. Neither did the gate keeper. He just looked round for a moment … only just a moment … and when he looked back someone had stuck it by the door.'

'Open it, my Lady,' suggested M'um Margot. 'Then you'll know. You may go, Tor.'

'Yes, M'um Margot,' said Tor regretfully, obviously hoping to hear the letter read. He shut the door behind him.

Ethel broke the seal and unfolded the letter. The paper was good quality parchment but yellowed at the edges, as though it had been stored for a long time before it had been used. M'um Margot looked carefully down at the store list, as though to indicate if Ethel wished it to be private she would not inquire.

The letter was brief.

My dear Ethel,

There is smoke in the Coasttown and ships on the sea. The T'manians have come. I will help if I can.

Alice.

Ethel sat without moving. It couldn't be true. It couldn't. The world couldn't shatter as fast as this.

T'manians ...

'Bad news?' asked M'um Margot gently beside her.

'The T'manians,' said Ethel stupidly. 'The T'manians are coming.'

'But ... but how do you know?'

'The letter ...' Ethel halted. How could she explain M'um Alice to M'um Margot? 'It's from a friend,' she went on quickly. 'From a lookout high on the hills. The T'manians are at the Coasttown.'

'Are you sure? Is this friend trustworthy?'

'Yes,' said Ethel quietly.

M'um Margot calculated quickly. 'It takes four hours to walk here from Coasttown. Or even less ...'

'Maybe they won't come here …' said Ethel hopefully. 'Maybe they'll stay at Coasttown or travel another road …'

'They'll loot Coasttown and send their loot to the ships,' said M'um Margot calmly. 'Then they'll take the main road inland. And that leads to here. The T'manians want land. They want farms. They won't stay in Coasttown.'

'But …' Ethel faltered. There was no way around it. The T'manians would be here …

'You are sure about this friend of yours?' insisted M'um Margot.

'Yes,' said Ethel, for suddenly she was.

'Then we have to hurry,' said M'um Margot.

'Yes.' Suddenly reality hit like a fist in the face. 'Grand Marshal Kevin,' she said. 'We have to tell him! He'll know what to do, how we can defend ourselves! Thank goodness we have Grand Marshal Kevin! We must call the villagers in from the farms! They must bring everything they need to the safety of the Hall …' She hurried from the room, M'um Margot behind her.

'T'manians!' Grand Marshal Kevin's bright round face seemed to shrink, like an apple that had been stored too long. 'Coming here? No, girl … I mean, my Lady. You must be mistaken. The T'manians would never come to a place like this, not after all these years, so far up the coast …'

'I'm not wrong!' cried Ethel. She waved the letter. 'I arranged a lookout.'

'You arranged a lookout? Without consulting me! That was wrong, very wrong, my Lady.' Grand Marshal Kevin was indignant. 'I'm in charge of the defences here. Lookouts are to be arranged then I should do the arranging. When I was in the service of King Dennis no one ever thought of …'

'Surely that's of no matter now,' said M'um Margot quietly.

'Yes!' cried Ethel. 'The T'manians will be here! We've got four hours to get ready! To defend ourselves!'

'Four hours!' stammered Grand Marshal Kevin. 'But … but the walls aren't finished.'

'I don't think they'll wait for us to finish the walls,' said M'um Margot dryly.

Ethel stared at her. M'um Margot had changed. No, she hadn't changed, that was the strange thing. Just when you'd have expected her to be different, she was just the same as she had always been, organised and matter-of-fact. But this wasn't a tally of the storerooms now. This was war!

'No. No — of course not.' Grand Marshal Kevin

seemed to take hold of himself. 'You are right … of course you are right. We must act at once!'

Ethel let out her breath in relief. Of course Grand Marshal Kevin knew what to do.

'Stevens, call the guard!' announced Grand Marshal Kevin. 'We must go at once!'

'Go? Go where?' cried Ethel.

'To the Far Mountain Stronghold of course. To ask for assistance. More troops, more guards, more swords and shields!'

'But it will take you a day's ride to get to Far Mountain! Maybe more. The T'manians will be here by then!'

'Lady, be sensible!' said Grand Marshal Kevin. 'We can't hold off an attack ourselves! We don't have the means! Even the walls aren't finished.'

'But you said …'

'Well, never mind that now,' said Grand Marshal Kevin hurriedly. 'The sooner I set off, the sooner we'll be back — with reinforcements! You can be sure that we'll bring reinforcements — Stevens, there you are! Call the guard together. We must leave at once!'

'But you can't take the guard!' cried Ethel.

'Of course I must, Lady! There are T'manians about! I must get through to Far Mountain safely if I'm to bring help to you. In two days I promise — three at most, or four …'

'No.'

Grand Marshal Kevin hesitated at the sound of Ethel's voice. 'My Lady?'

'No, you will not take the guard. We need the guard here. They are the only ones who have ever fought the T'manians.'

Grand Marshal Kevin's face stilled. 'They are my guard, my Lady,' he said quietly. 'Not yours.'

'They stay,' said Ethel.

Grand Marshal Kevin smiled. Ethel had never seen Grand Marshal Kevin smile like that before. 'Call the guard then, my Lady. Let's see if they will stay with you, or come with me.'

Ethel glanced at M'um Margot. M'um Margot nodded, and slipped out the door. A moment later she reappeared, with the noise of many feet behind her.

Ethel gazed at the line of guards. There were five of them, tall men like the Grand Marshal, and the herald and standard bearer, too. They wore swords, and tunics, and their hands were calloused in different ways from a farmer's hands, or a tanner's.

'Will you explain or will I?' she asked Grand Marshal Kevin.

'You explain. You are the Lady,' said Grand Marshal Kevin. His voice was polite.

Ethel watched the faces of the men. Why did it seem so normal for M'um Alice to look down on her, while these men made her feel so small?

There was no time to waste feeling insignificant, she told herself. She held her chin high. 'The T'manians are invading Coasttown,' she announced, as calmly as she could. 'The Grand Marshal believes that the best tactics are to get reinforcements from Far Mountain. He would like you to go with him,' she lifted her chin a fraction higher, 'to hold his hand perhaps when it gets dark. But I'm ordering you to stay here, instead, to help with the defences here, though the Grand Marshal,' she shot him a scornful look, 'may go if he likes. Do you understand me?'

No one answered. The men glanced at the Grand Marshal.

The Grand Marshal smiled his strange new smile again. 'I think you will find that my men follow where I lead,' he answered softly. 'I'm the Grand Marshal, my dear.' He paused, the smile deepening. 'I mean, my Lady.'

Ethel glanced round at the guard. None met her eyes.

'But you gave me your word!' cried Ethel. 'You've lived here all these months, eaten our food!'

'For which we thank you, my Lady,' said the Grand Marshal. 'But now it's time to go.'

'Did you ever intend to fight if the invaders came?' asked Ethel quietly.

One of the men grinned. The Grand Marshal shook his head. 'Why would T'manians come here, so far up the coast? They had small enough pickings last time. No metal — who wants to haul pumpkins to the coast? Although it seems now they have come. No girl. I've done enough fighting not to want more. Oh, I'd have built your walls for you, given enough time. But only a fool fights when they don't have to.' He hesitated for a moment. 'Look girl. I won't stay for you. But I will give you advice. Good advice. I may not have done all I said I did back in your Hall, but I have fought the T'manians before.'

We don't want your advice! screamed Ethel's mind. But her voice was silent.

'My best advice — though you probably won't take it — is for you to tell your people to take what they can, and escape now. Otherwise they'll be killed, or kept or sold as slaves.'

'But where should we run to!' cried Ethel.

The Grand Marshal shrugged. 'But if you do decide to fight,' he continued, 'keep your people fighting. If they start to run they're lost. Armies need leaders. If one person runs everyone will run. But if one person leads, then … maybe … your people will, too.'

'Anything else?' asked Ethel quietly.

The Grand Marshal shook his head. 'You have no weapons,' he said. 'No one with any experience. As I said, my best advice, my dear, is to go now, taking what you can. I'm sure Far Mountain will shelter you and M'um Margot, even if it doesn't have room for the villagers.'

For the first time Grand Marshal Kevin met her eyes.

'I'm not a villain, Lady. I'm just a man who has seen too much fighting, just as my men have.'

'Then why didn't you turn farmer? Tanner? Builder?' cried Ethel.

'Us? Farmers!' The Grand Marshal laughed. He was still laughing as they left the room.

Ethel watched him go.

'Just like that,' she whispered. 'As soon as there's danger he's gone ... What do we do now?'

'We make do with what we've got,' said M'um Margot.

It was almost as though they were back at the stocktaking — four barrels of salt fish, eighteen smoked legs of geep ...

'Sound the bells,' said Ethel quietly. 'Call in the villagers. Call everyone together in the forecourt. You're right. We must make do with what we've got.'

The forecourt was full — men in shepherd's aprons jostled with men in tanning leathers; women in farmer's skirts next to cooks and silversmiths. Ethel watched them helplessly. She had never felt younger, never felt more alone. What was the use of being able to ride a unicorn now? Did it make her a better leader? Did it tell her how to harness villagers into a fighting force to repel the T'manians?

Ethel felt the unicorn's damp nose against her arm. It gave her confidence. She was the Lady of the Unicorn. She must know what to do! She vaulted quietly onto his back. At least up here she could see and be seen.

'Villagers, farmers, people of the Hall ...' her voice shook. To her surprise the courtyard was suddenly silent, the faces, round as plates along the sideboard, looking up at her.

'The T'manians are coming!' Fool, she told herself — they know that, that's why they're here. 'We have two choices. We can fight, or we can run.

'If we run, we leave everything — our harvest, our land, our homes. And even then the T'manians may catch up with us and make us slaves, or worse.'

'There's nothing worse,' said a voice.

'Oh yes, there is,' said someone else.

Ethel ignored them. Somehow now she had started to speak it was easy to keep on, as though she was no longer Ethel, as though for the first time she *was* the Lady of the Unicorn. She could feel the power seep into her — the power of their expectations, the power of their love. Even if it was for the Lady and not for her, it was still there.

'This is OUR land!' For the first time her voice rang clear. 'Let anyone who wants to leave, leave it now! Now! While there's still time — perhaps — to run!'

Ethel looked slowly around.

No one moved.

'Then we will fight!' she said.

'But ... but how ...' the voice was bewildered, not antagonistic. Somehow it broke the tension. Ethel grinned.

'With our hoes and rakes and kitchen knives — with everything we have!'

'But they have spears and shields.' Again the voice was only questioning, as though *of course* the Lady would know the answer.

And somehow the answer came. From books? From stories that she'd heard? Or because she *was* the Lady. The unicorn shuffled slightly. Ethel held him still. 'They have their spears,' said Ethel. 'But we have something else. We love this land. We have to fight for it. They don't.

'And we have something else. We know our own villages. We know every track and tree. And that's what we'll use to defeat the T'manians!'

'What about Grand Marshal Kevin?' came another voice from the back of the crowd. 'Where is he? Where are the guards?'

Ethel gritted her teeth. 'The Grand Marshal has ...' she stopped. She couldn't say that the Grand Marshal had fled, announcing the case was hopeless. But she had to say something. They were waiting ...

'The Grand Marshal has gone to get reinforcements,' came a voice behind her. 'He'll be back when he can.' Ethel stared. It was the youngest of the Grand Marshal guard's, the one who had brought the message from M'um Alice, Tor Underhill. 'Till he returns,' he turned to Ethel. 'I'll help the Lady organise our defences here.'

Tears stung Ethel's eyes. 'We have three hours to get ready,' she said instead. 'Maybe four.'

The crowd was quiet as she spoke.

The water clock dripped slowly in the courtyard. A cart creaked in through the gateway and then another, piled high with blankets, pumpkins, beds, sacks of seed and sheaves of hay — everything that could be gathered in was piled around the courtyard, with M'um Margot still with her tally book, accounting for it all.

'Weapons,' demanded Ethel.

Tor Underhill nodded. 'I'll see to it, my Lady. It's best that everyone uses the ones they know. A soldier can use a sword because he's been trained to them for years. But a farmer knows the balance of her hoe or rake. And the blacksmith knows the feel of hammers …'

'Tor?'

'Yes, my Lady?'

'Why didn't you leave with the others?'

Tor shrugged. 'I had to choose,' he said. 'Either be loyal to you, or to the Grand Marshal. I met the Grand Marshal only six months before we came here, my Lady. I had no reason to be loyal to him.'

'And you had to me?'

Tor nodded. 'I was brought up around here, my Lady. My family has always followed the Lady of the Unicorns.'

'Oh,' said Ethel. 'Have you ever fought the T'manians, Tor?'

'No, my Lady. But I've listened to the other guards' stories. And the Grand Marshal taught me sword craft. I can drill troops, my Lady.'

Ethel gazed out at the crowded courtyard again. 'If only there was some other way to defend ourselves.'

'If this was a castle,' said Tor slowly. 'We could pour boiling oil down on the invaders. Or rocks …'

'But this land is flat.' Ethel shook her head. 'If only there was some way to trap them before they got to the Hall, some way to …' Suddenly she stopped. 'Tor!'

'Yes, my Lady.'

'I've had an idea. Maybe it's a silly idea.'

'No idea is silly now, my Lady,' said Tor seriously.

'Maybe …' said Ethel slowly. 'Just maybe … it will work …'

The clock in the courtyard dripped down onto the rocks. The moisture seeped into the crevices, feeding the watercress and swamp dock that grew below the clock.

Two hours. Three hours. Four.

'Any sign?' demanded Ethel.

'No, my Lady,' said M'um Margot calmly.

'The lookouts?'

'In place up on the roof, my Lady.'

'The hay?'

'Pul the Shepherd says it's scattered, my Lady.'

'The barricades?'

M'um Margot nodded. 'Everything we could lay our hands on, my Lady. It's all piled up before the Hall. Tor is drilling,' she gave a slight smile. 'Drilling the troops out front.'

The Lady's troops, thought Ethel. Farmers and bakers and geepherds, with hoes and rakes and sticks …

The barricades would keep no one out — only the Grand Marshal's walls might have done that. But they would at least provide shelter against the spears till the T'manians drew close.

Suddenly Ethel's mind was blank. There had to be more that they could do. But she couldn't think. She had to think, thought Ethel desperately. She had to make decisions for her people.

'Then get everyone together,' said Ethel's voice, the Lady's voice. 'In lines behind the barricade.'

They waited outside the Hall behind the piled up firewood and furniture and carts. The sun beat down, shadowless.

'Send the children in for water,' ordered Ethel. 'Tell them to bring buckets and cups so everyone can drink. Bring water for the unicorn, too.' The unicorn snorted beside her. The activity had upset him. He tossed his head restlessly. His tail flicked, though the day was still too cool for flies.

Four hours, M'um Margot had said. It took a man four hours to walk from Coasttown to the Hall. But these men would be moving swiftly, hoping to arrive before the alarm went out, before fleeing Coasttowners brought their message to the Hall.

'Five hours,' muttered Ethel. 'It's been five hours since we had word.'

'Then they'll be here soon,' said M'um Margot calmly beside her.

'M'um Margot ...' whispered Ethel.

'Yes?' answered M'um Margot.

'Nothing. It's just ... it's just I wish the Grand Marshal were here ... Or not the Grand Marshal — someone who really knew how to lead ...'

'You're managing, pet,' said M'um Margot. 'I mean, my Lady.'

'That's the first time you've called me "my Lady" since the message came,' said Ethel irrelevantly.

M'um Margot grinned. A lock of hair had slipped from her headdress, rusty against her indoors face. 'Maybe I had to keep reminding myself that you really were the Lady before. But you're the Lady now well enough. You're doing fine, pet. You're doing fine.'

Suddenly down the road a dark grey plume of smoke twisted towards the sky. A farm roof set on fire, thought Ethel. The T'manians were nearly at the village.

Someone muttered fearfully behind her. The whispers rose and fell along the lines — 'They're here, they're here, they're here ...'

'They're here, my Lady,' said Tor unnecessarily.

'Send the children into the Hall,' ordered Ethel. 'Joel Blacksmith, tell them to fetch the oil.'

'Yes, my Lady,' said Joel Blacksmith.

Then she saw them.

They were far away still, just past the hills between

the Hall and the coast. Like earwigs thought Ethel, not like people yet at all. The sun glinted on their spears, the metal garlands round their necks and arms. It was like something in a book, thought Ethel. It was all just the same as everyone described, except here it was real.

It didn't feel real. It felt as though you could turn the page and it would all be over. If only she could just turn the page and skip this bit. Or put the book away and say, 'I don't want to read this anymore.'

But this was real.

Could she hear them? Surely not at this distance — and yet she could. The muffled thump of many feet, the jangle of armour. But no voices. That was the most ominous aspect. The silence. There was too much silence. As though the birds too knew there would be a battle, as though even the animals had retreated.

A muffled creak passed behind her. Ethel didn't turn. That would be the oil pots being dragged down to the village where the straw was laid. She could smell them, hot in the cool air.

Closer, closer, closer — the T'manians moved together, like a tortoise or a snake, thought Ethel, but you could see that they were men now, although they were still too distant to see their faces. No, thought Ethel suddenly. They weren't men. You couldn't hurt someone if you thought of them as men. They were just the enemy.

'They're nearly at the village, my Lady,' someone whispered, as though the T'manians might hear if they spoke any louder.

'Not yet,' said Ethel. She stared at the T'manians till her eyes began to blur. They were short — even from here she could see that — their shoulders broad and their heads entirely hairless. Ethel wondered if their women were hairless, too. Their skins gleamed slightly silver, an oil perhaps, to protect their skin from the sea glare.

Ethel could hear her pulse ringing in her head. When should I give the order? she thought desperately. What if I get it wrong? When? When? When? In fifty breaths' time maybe — she listened to her breathing, began to count.

One, two, three …

You could see the spears now, high above their heads, like saplings that had lost their leaves. Metal spears, and spears of fire-hardened wood, almost as lethal.

Twenty, twenty-one …

The first T'manians disappeared hidden between the cottages.

Thirty-two, thirty-three …

Now, thought Ethel, now … any longer and they may separate, pillage the cottages before descending on the Hall.

'Now!' she yelled.

Immediately a pigeon shot into the air; and then another and another.

Ethel stared down at the village.

Nothing happened.

What was wrong? Was the oil too cool to light? Was the straw too damp to fire. Surely there must be smoke soon. Surely …

Then someone screamed.

It was a long scream, on and on and on. Another came and then another — the village was full of screams.

Someone ran along the road, writhing and turning, their hair on fire. Others boiled out into the fields, throwing themselves onto the cool damp earth, rolling, rolling, rolling …

'It was a good plan,' said M'um Margot quietly. 'Filling the streets with straw then pouring hot oil down and firing it. We should stop a lot of them that way.'

'It was Tor's idea,' said Ethel. 'He said they pour oil down from the castle walls onto the invaders. I wasn't sure if it would really work. I thought there would be smoke.'

'Not from burning oil and straw,' said M'um Margot. 'Not from this distance. It just looks like a heat haze in the air. Ah, there's smoke now — one of the cottages must have caught. Now they'll be running towards the pits.'

Like M'um Alice's pits, thought Ethel, only covered with wet straw, so they looked just like the road, but wouldn't burn. She wondered suddenly if M'um Alice was watching the battle from her hilltop. Could she see her on her unicorn? But surely it was too far away for that.

Suddenly the screaming changed.

'Your plan worked, pet,' approved M'um Margot.

'But how many have been caught?' whispered Ethel. 'How many are still left?'

'We'll know soon enough,' said M'um Margot.

Someone gave a sob of fear in the line behind. The sound stopped abruptly as though they were ashamed.

How long could it take for the surviving T'manians to leave the village? wondered Ethel. Maybe, maybe there were no survivors. Maybe they'd all been trapped or burnt. She turned to M'um Margot, then stopped.

The first of the T'manians appeared between the cottages, and then another ... and another. They were close enough to see their round chins now, the smudges on the arms and legs, their armlets and their shields.

So many, thought Ethel desperately. There were still so many. The unicorn stamped beside her, alarmed by the screams. She patted him till he was still.

'We must have got half of them,' said Tor beside her.

Ethel nodded. Even half were so many. They looked determined, undeterred, as though they met burning oil and pit traps every month.

Of course, realised Ethel, those were the tools of war. You survived them or you didn't. And you grew used to them. You couldn't scare the T'manians with oil or traps.

The T'manians drew together — like a beetle, thought Ethel, a beetle with many legs and antennae waving at the sky. Someone gave a signal at the front.

The beetle began to march again.

A villager muttered in the lines behind. The muttering spread like melted butter down a hearth cake.

Ethel gripped her spear. It felt strange in her hand. It had hung in the Hall above the hearth. She wondered who had used it before. How long ago? Another Lady of the Unicorn perhaps? Then it should know her hand. But it felt strange.

'Listen!' she cried. The words were lost in the muttering behind. 'Listen!' she cried again, and now someone took up the cry — 'Listen to the Lady! Listen!'

Ethel tried to keep her voice steady. 'The time is nearly here! Remember! If one of us runs the rest may run but if we run we will be killed. If we stand we may be killed. But at least if we stand together we have a chance.'

The muttering stopped. 'If we die the enemy gets our land. But if we win …' Tears filled Ethel's eyes suddenly. Who would give *her* courage? Who was there for her to lean on?

'Advance when I give the order!' cried Ethel. She mounted the unicorn. His coat was warm against her legs. She gripped the reins.

The enemy advanced, still beetle-like, steady and determined. Then suddenly the leader signalled again. The clump spread out to become a line, three deep perhaps, or four, curving slightly at the edges. They intended to surround the Hall, Ethel realised. Kill or be captured …

The line advanced. The unicorn snorted and twisted his head.

So many … so many … so many …

When would it start? Would they charge? Or just keep walking steadily, strike them steadily, kill them steadily …

No, she decided. The leader would give a signal and they'd run, their spears held low, their sword arms raised. And those behind her might run too. For who could stand when armed T'manians poured towards them?

They had to advance instead! It would give her people confidence if they were the attackers instead of waiting for the spears! She glanced at the people behind her — Tor with his sword, waiting for the

Lady's order, M'um Margot with a kitchen knife, Gary Tanner with his sharp, steel scraper, the farmers with their hoes and potato forks …

Would it really make any difference in the end?

The unicorn stood steady beneath her, his breath soft and even. At least he wasn't afraid.

Ethel opened her mouth to call the charge.

Someone screamed. It was a different scream from the one before. This was a scream of terror.

Ethel turned.

It was, what was her name? One of the women from the dairy. She pointed at the T'manians — no, not at the T'manians. She pointed up beyond them to the hill behind.

Something was coming from behind the hill. People, many people. Were they people? Ethel squinted into the sun. The shapes were wrong for people. Too tall, too small, the wrong colours — no one was as tall as that, except M'um Alice, and …

A cloud shifted across the sun and M'um Alice lumbered into view.

She wasn't alone. The others were all with her — all the people from the clearing that moonlit night and more besides, as though they'd spread the word through all the forest and the hills and plains. There was the white-faced giant, taller than M'um Alice; the old woman carried on his back; and other giants, thin lips in long chinned faces, and a dragon creature. Was there really a dragon in the forest ... or was it human, too? And others, so many others, the hidden people facing daylight for their friend.

Was she their friend? Not yet, thought Ethel. But M'um Alice was their friend. They'd come for her.

Slowly they came forward, steadily across the plain, M'um Alice in the lead. Something scurried at her side. Hingram, Ethel realised. She could see him clearly now. He stopped, and as though he sensed her too, he lifted up his head and howled.

Caroooooooooooooo!

The sound filled the hollow air. Another person screamed and pointed. One of the T'manians turned around, and stared ...

'Attack!' shouted Ethel.

No one moved.

'Attack!' she yelled again

'But ... but, my Lady — the monsters!' The voice was low. An enemy they could face. But not the monsters.

'They'll fight for us! Don't you understand? They are our friends!'

There was no way to convince them. Or only one way ... *Armies need leaders.*

Ethel dug her heels into the side of the unicorn. He reared, almost toppling her. He yelled in challenge to the horses facing them.

It was the first time she had ever heard him make a sound.

And then he charged.

She could hear his hooves against the dust brown grass. She could hear his breath panting in her ears.

There was no other sound.

And then the cries began behind her — a battlecry from Tor and M'um Margot's warlike scream (who would have thought that M'um Margot could scream like that?). Fifty cries, a hundred and the sound of running feet.

Ethel faced the enemy.

But the enemy had turned. They paid no attention to the villagers with their rakes and knives. They stared at the monsters coming from behind.

Their line broke without a sound. They ran, but not like an army ran. They ran towards the villagers, their spears cast down in their terror to be away.

The monsters shambled behind them.

Ethel pulled frantically at the unicorn's reins. He halted, shying to one side. Someone ran in front of her — Gary Tanner, his rake raised high, striking at the fleeing men. Others came after him, their weapons raised. There was a new scent in the air, of blood and steel and hatred.

'Stop them!' Ethel turned. 'There's no need to fight now! The T'manians just want to escape! Stop!' she cried, but her voice was lost in the yells and screams. 'Stop!'

A man lunged against the unicorn, sending him skittering to one side. For a moment Ethel thought he was attacking her, then she realised he was unconscious, blood seeping from his skull.

'Stop it!' she shrieked, and this time the unicorn rose with her cry, his hooves flying towards the sky. But still the fight went on.

'She said, stop it!' The voice boomed across the battlefield. Ethel glanced around.

It was M'um Alice. She loomed above the fighters, twice as high as the tallest of them, her hands wider than two men's heads, her voice louder than the cries of pain. Why did she look so much larger here, thought Ethel wildly, than on her hilltop? Because here you saw her surrounded by the world of ordinary sizes and proportions ...

M'um Alice reached down. She grasped Gary Tanner in one giant hand and held him high; the other reached for a smooth headed T'manian. His metal necklace swung against his chest as she shook him like a rat.

'Lay down your arms,' boomed M'um Alice. 'Every one of you! I mean *now*!'

There was silence. A rake clinked, a knife thudded on the grass. Then suddenly all over the battlefield men and women were laying down their hoes, their plough blades, Solvig Sweeper's broom. Someone groaned, and then was still.

M'um Alice lowered the men to the ground. Gary Tanner blinked, his legs buckling as he collapsed onto the grass. His face was green.

The bearded invader recovered faster. He glanced once at Gary Tanner, once at M'um Alice looming above them, then he was running, running, running swerving through the silent crowd.

'Catch him!' someone yelled.

'No!' cried Ethel. 'Let him go! Let them all go!'

And suddenly the field was full of running T'manians, their weapons left behind them, their feet thudding on the flattened grass, back to the road and to the sea.

'We should go after them,' someone called.

'No!' said Ethel again. 'Let them run! Let them tell everyone what happens to T'manians here!'

'The monsters get them,' someone muttered, looking uneasily across to the hill.

'The monsters,' whispered another and the whisper

spread. 'The monsters, the monsters, the monsters ...'
Ethel followed their gaze.

The people of the forest had stopped advancing. Like
M'um Alice they looked even more different out here
on the plain, their strangeness accentuated by the
ordinariness around them. Were screams and battles
normal? Maybe it was the gentle peace of the forest
people that was strange, and not their faces ...

'M'um Alice?' said Ethel unsteadily.

M'um Alice strode towards her. 'Are you all right,
child?' she asked. Her voice low.

Ethel nodded. There seemed no words to say. 'Thank
you,' she said finally. 'I ... I'm sorry for what I said ...'

M'um Alice smiled, her eyes intent on Ethel's. As
though she didn't dare look to either side, thought
Ethel and see the revulsion on other people's faces.

'We told you in the forest,' said M'um Alice gently.
'We help our friends.'

'Thank you,' said Ethel again. For some reason the
world seemed strangely clear, the sounds retreating to a
distant buzzing in her ears.

'Catch her,' said a voice — M'um Margot's, but very
far away ...

The bookroom was quiet when she opened her eyes.
The books piled on their shelves, just as they should be,

with the bags of mint bush and garlic to keep away the silverfish, the high wooden ceiling free of cobwebs — M'um Margot would never allow a cobweb.

'Here,' said M'um Margot. Something warm touched Ethel's lips. She sipped.

'M'um Alice?'

'I'm here,' said a voice.

'She carried you in,' said M'um Margot.

'My unicorn?'

'He's in the courtyard munching thistles,' said M'um Margot. 'He's safe. Everyone's safe. I've had the wounded carried in. They're in the Hall.'

'The wounded?' Ethel tried to sit up. M'um Margot pushed a pillow behind her.

'Don't you worry now, pet,' she said. 'I mean, my Lady. There are none that won't heal with a little nursing.'

'How many are there?'

M'um Margot counted on her fingers. 'George the Weaver, he took a nasty blow on the head, and Eric the Binder, Gary Tanner fetched him a blow accidentally with his rake. He's got a cut right down his arm but it will heal, it will heal, and Tor took a blow as well. Little Agnes from the farm by the creek, she's hurt the worst — the T'manians got her before they reached the field, the child must have been hiding. A few others, nothing to what might have been, thanks to M'um Alice and her friends.'

M'um Alice said nothing.

Ethel sipped the drink again. It was bitter and hot, one of M'um Margot's 'good for you' teas, but she felt stronger with every sip.

'There's one who would speak to you, when you're feeling better,' said M'um Margot slowly. She met Ethel's eyes. Her look was strange.

'One of the wounded?' asked Ethel.

M'um Margot nodded. 'Do you feel strong enough?' she asked.

Ethel struggled to her feet. She felt silly to be so weak now. 'Of course.' She looked over at M'um Alice.

'Off you go,' said M'um Alice. 'I'll be all right here.'

The Hall stank of blood and fear. M'um Margot had been busy, ordering hay beds for the wounded, salves and bandages to tend the wounds, and boiled strips of old petticoat that had been left to dry in the sun and rolled with lavender flowers to keep them pure, pots of powdered basil and calendula and comfrey root, all the silly things that M'um Margot had collected and that didn't seem so silly now.

'Over here,' instructed M'um Margot.

Ethel trod between the pallets. Old Bertram, his eyes shut with the pain, his arm and one side bandaged. Little Agnes from the farm by the creek.

Why had the T'manians bothered with a tiny child?

Ethel wondered whether to smile, to reassure or comfort. But the wounded were buried in their world of pain.

M'um Margot stopped. Ethel looked down.

A man lay on the pallet before her. His skin was smudged with silver, whatever lotion he'd been wearing partially cleaned away. His face must have been bloody, for long gashes ran down his cheek as though they had been cut with a rake perhaps, rather than a sword. Now it was clean and the gashes covered with a layer of salve, like sliced strawberries set in jelly, thought Ethel, her stomach lurching suddenly. His side was bandaged too. His face paled as he tried to sit, then fell back among the straw.

Ethel stared at his blue, clear eyes, the round, bare skull, the iron around his neck, the silver skin.

This was the enemy.

For a moment M'um Margot met her eyes. M'um Margot, who had always been so loyal to her and to her people. M'um Margot had brought a T'manian inside the Hall.

The man gasped, as if he tried to speak. Slowly Ethel nodded. M'um Margot smiled an almost smile.

'I'll leave you with him,' she said. 'He wishes to speak to you alone.'

Ethel knelt by the man's side. 'Speak,' she said.

The man frowned, as though it hurt to concentrate through his pain. 'I beg a favour,' he gasped. His accent was strange but intelligible. 'Oh gracious Lady ...'

'Don't waste your strength,' said Ethel. 'If you have something to ask of me, just ask.'

'I would like to stay,' said the man simply.

Ethel stared. 'You mean stay here?'

The man nodded.

'But ... but you're our enemy. You can't stay here. We must send you to Coasttown. They have a prison there. You can be ransomed. Don't worry. We don't keep prisoners slaves.'

'I wish to stay here,' said the man. His voice was even weaker.

'But why?' cried Ethel. 'This isn't your home. We're not your people!'

'I have no home,' said the man. 'The water covered all my island. I came here hoping for a home. No one will ransom me. I was loyal to my leader. I didn't run with the others. I stayed till I was struck down. Now I would be loyal to you.'

'But ...'

'I would be loyal,' promised the man. His eyes closed, bruised smudges in his too-white face. His breathing deepened.

Ethel stood and walked back through the Hall. Who are friends and who are enemies? she thought. How can you ever know?

A hand clutched her skirt and she looked down. It was Tor Underhill. His skull and thigh were bandaged.

'Tor! What happened! How badly are you hurt?'

Tor shook his head, as though his wounds were irrelevant. 'The monsters ...' he said urgently. 'Lady, have the monsters gone?'

'What monsters?' asked Ethel, though she knew.

'We were just about to fight ... then the monsters came ... and we attacked ... and something struck me ... there were monsters all along the hill ...'

'Don't worry,' said Ethel gently. 'They fought for us.'

'For us, my Lady?' The pain-thickened voice sounded confused. 'Then we've won.'

'We won,' said Ethel. 'We're safe. Go to sleep, Tor. We're all safe.'

M'um Margot met her in the courtyard. 'Will you let the T'manian stay?' she asked.

Ethel nodded. 'We've land to spare, if that's what he wants. Do you think I'm right?' she asked.

'I think so,' said M'um Margot.

'I'd better go,' said Ethel. 'M'um Alice will wonder where I am.'

M'um Margot shook her head. 'She's gone,' she said.

'Gone? But she can't have gone! I haven't thanked her properly! We have to bring her back! She must stay here!'

'Let her go, pet,' said M'um Margot softly. 'Help tend the wounded now. You can see her later.'

'But she saved us …'

'And now she wants to go. She can't stay here.'

'But …' Ethel stopped. *Have the monsters gone?* Tor Underhill had asked.

M'um Alice would always be a monster here.

Suddenly the unicorn snickered from his shelter in the corner of the yard. His horn glinted in the dusty orange light. His blue eyes, blue as eyes of the man who had once been an enemy, met hers across the cobbles.

Ethel looked at the unicorn who was her friend. If you put a unicorn with horses they'd stamp it to death. She was the girl who rode the unicorn. She was different, though her difference made her the Lady, not an outcast. The unicorn was different. And her other friends. Are only those who are different at ease with others who are different? she wondered. Maybe when you were born different you had to become wise.

And M'um Margot? Ethel smiled. Maybe some people just learn how to be wise. Or perhaps their differences didn't show …

'Take me with you when you visit her again,' said

M'um Margot softly. 'I would like to meet M'um Alice properly next time.'

Ethel nodded.

The world had seemed so simple when enemies were simply enemies, and giants sucked their victim's bones. The world was more confusing now. But for the first time she knew what it might mean to be the Lady.

The unicorn whinnied again. Ethel gazed up at the hill. There was M'um Alice trudging up the slope. Something dark scurried at her heels. Hingram, come to meet his friend away from the stares of other people.

Her friends. The monsters who were generous, the enemy who would now be loyal, the old woman who was strong.

Ethel looked back at M'um Margot. She was smiling, the smile of an old friend for a young one. 'Let's go in,' said Ethel. 'There's a lot to do.'

Things had changed in the past. Maybe tolerance could come once more. Somehow it no longer seemed so impossible that she, the Lady of the Unicorns, might lead her people once again.

They walked back into the Hall together.